MARK CAREW was born in [...]
near Sudbury, Suffolk. He studie[...]
College, London, and received a PhD in Cell Physiology
from Cambridge in 1995. After post docs in Cambridge
and North Carolina, he worked as a medical writer before
joining Kingston University where he is an Associate
Professor. His stories have appeared in print and online in
literary magazines. *The Book of Alexander* is his first novel.

THE
BOOK OF
ALEXANDER

MARK CAREW

CROMER

PUBLISHED BY SALT PUBLISHING 2018

2 4 6 8 10 9 7 5 3 1

First published in Great Britain in 2018 by
Salt Publishing Ltd
12 Norwich Road, Cromer, Norfolk NR27 0AX United Kingdom

www.saltpublishing.com

Salt Publishing Limited Reg. No. 5293401

A CIP catalogue record for this book is available from the British Library

ISBN 978 1 78463 132 1 (Paperback edition)
ISBN 978 1 78463 133 8 (Electronic edition)

Typeset in Neacademia by Salt Publishing

Printed and bound in Great Britain by Clays Ltd, Elcograf S.p.A

Salt Publishing Limited is committed to responsible forest management.
This book is made from Forest Stewardship Council™ certified paper.

To all the dreamers – it's hard work

CHAPTER 1

THIS WAS ONE of the most remarkable cases I've worked on. It was the Monday of the third week of October, the days were cooling, and I was already missing the last of the Indian summer evenings in the garden with my wife. I was settled at the kitchen table with a cup of tea, musing about my next job, and speculating about its details, which I would learn very soon. The doorbell rang. The man on the doorstep was expected; we had an appointment. He shook my hand and engaged me with a flashing smile. He was one of those middle-aged men, fifty or so, with hair flecked grey in places, and crow's feet under laughing brown eyes, but who still managed to look young, keeping himself slim and boyish. He smiled a lot, shook my hand with a firm grip, and was polite as he entered the house.

I hung up his jacket for him, and he sat down at the table opposite me. I offered him a drink and he decided on a cup of green tea, which my wife likes every now and then. As the kettle boiled, I listened to his request.

He wanted me to watch a young man to whom he referred as someone of whom the family had taken notice. I enquired further, and it turned out that his daughter was interested in this young man, whose name was Alexander, and my client wanted to know more about him. His daughter, Penny, was quite taken with her boyfriend, but the family name needed to be protected. I exchanged nods with my affable client. Of all the reasons people give me to have someone watched, this was one of the most benign: a protective father looking out for his daughter, and no doubt his own interests.

My client simply wanted Alexander watched, and for Alexander not to know he was being watched, and for me to write down my impressions of what he was like. In return, the client would pay me a handsome fee for my report, to be deposited at a bank. He wrote the address of the bank on a piece of paper I found for him, and I stuck it on the fridge with a magnet. The branch of the bank was in the middle of the city, next to the main post office.

I told him that I would hand-deliver the report to the bank myself. I anticipated I would need a period of about two weeks to complete it.

My client was impressed, and wrote down the name of the bank manager, a business acquaintance, who could be trusted to receive the report. He also wrote down the name of the street Alexander lived in. He didn't know the exact address, as his daughter had been vague about it. He didn't have a photograph of Alexander, either, but said that he was young, tall, and handsome, with dark brown hair. However, this information came from his estranged wife rather than his daughter.

I pressed for more information about Alexander, anxious to understand the sort of world I might be getting into. Even in this celebrated university city there were places and people that the police were wary of visiting. I didn't particularly want to get mixed up with anything heavy.

My client sipped the hot green tea I had placed in front of him, and told me a little more about Alexander, in the process putting my fears to rest. Alexander was a student of fine art at the university. As was typical for people in that line of work ("If it can be called that!" laughed my client), according to the daughter he stayed in his house a lot, and was working on a grand project. The aim of this grand project had not been disclosed; my client was intrigued about it and wished to know more. He also wanted to gain a general idea about Alexander's character. Marriage had not been spoken of, but it was as well to be prepared. As a father, he might need to head off a prospective engagement if Alexander was deemed to be unsuitable.

I thought about the sum of money on offer: it was very good, easy money for what the client wanted delivered. Jobs don't grow on trees in my line of work, and the money (it's always about the money) was a very big draw. I might even be able to surprise my wife by giving her a foreign holiday.

I agreed to take the case. I reckoned that my proposed period of two weeks' surveillance was about right. If necessary, and depending on the outcome of the report, we could meet again, and I would take the case further if needed. Hiring a private detective to watch a man is not against the law, but in my experience it can become something of a fetish for the client, as well as unhealthy for the detective, who may develop a propensity for making things up to appease the client in order to continue taking his money.

My client agreed to my suggested modus operandi, so I slid a piece of paper detailing my terms and conditions across the table and left him to study it. In the small downstairs room I used as an office, I filled in my standard contract with details of my client's name (Mr Anthony Travis), the rates for the work, the details of the deliverables, how payment was to be made by bank transfer and the deadline for completion. It all looked very simple and straightforward.

When I returned, Mr Travis had signed my terms and conditions with a signature that flourished above but not below the line. I'd studied a course in graphology and recognised this as the signature of a sincere man.

I presented my client with the contract, which he proceeded to read fully, as businessmen are hard-wired to do. When he was satisfied with it, I went back to my office, and made a copy of the signed contract for him. He was most pleased, as was I, and I told him that I would be happy to start work the following morning. We shook hands. Then he left, skipping down the steps chuckling to himself.

In my ledger I noted the date and time of our meeting and assigned a new number to the case. I wrote the target's name, Alexander, on the front of a new manila folder in thick black pen and put the contract and Ts & Cs inside. My accountant expected close attention to such detail when we met for my annual financial health check.

By the time my wife returned, I had cleared the kitchen and made supper: a sausage and bean stew. We commented on the oddly warm autumn. She watched TV that evening, but I couldn't concentrate: I felt distracted, already starting to think about the case, and what Alexander might be like, and where he lived. I went to bed early.

I didn't sleep. I imagined Alexander as a young handsome man, a paintbrush in his hand, painting some very important work of art. My experience of art was chiefly informed by my experiences in the art room at school, where I remembered being criticised by a girl for only drawing straight lines. A real artist would be able to paint faces, and use colour in amazing ways, and would have an air of detached aloofness about his mighty brow.

But that was a silly caricature of an artist. What was an artist really like? Was he actually just like you and me, but with a single, special skill, like a pianist who could play the piano beautifully, but who still spoke with his mouth full at the table, and didn't wipe the toilet seat when he peed?

Sometimes on buses there's a screen which flickers every few seconds and shows the image from one of several cameras stationed around the vehicle. It's funny to look at yourself in the image, standing next to the other passengers, and after a while you forget that it's you standing there, and you blend in with the crowd: the third person objective viewpoint, just showing you what there is, with sound if you are clever. That man who looks like me, the one standing with his hand on the pole, pushing the button to bring the bus to a halt at the next stop, or, for that matter, the man lying now in bed, thinking too hard about this stuff, imagining that he is a fly on the wall looking down on himself. What's that man really like – and does he even know the answer to that?

I couldn't fault Mr Travis for wanting to know about Alexander, because looks can be deceiving, as surely any man over forty could tell you. What Mr Travis wanted was an in-depth character assessment of his daughter's beau, which was exactly what I intended to provide.

CHAPTER 2

ALEXANDER'S ROAD WAS easy to find the next day, which was a Tuesday. Finding his exact house took a little longer. On one side of the road was a line of old, possibly Victorian, buildings. On the other side were newer houses, and slap in the middle of them, rather oddly, was a petrol garage: the street was busy with cars stopping to fill up, or to visit its little shop. I parked my car a few streets away, near the river and a rowing club, and walked up to Adelaide Road, where I stood outside a pub called the Hay Wain and surveyed the scene. Which one of these houses was Alexander's? Did he rent, or did he own his house? Did he live in one of the new or the old houses?

My questions were soon answered. A young man on a bicycle rode up from the direction of the river, the same route I had taken, turned left on the road, hopped up on to the pavement outside the post office and headed down to the old houses opposite the garage. He stopped outside a house with a blue door; the brakes on his bicycle made a loud squawk. He was tallish, but under six foot, and had long, floppy hair. I walked up a side street so I could get a better look. He unlocked the blue gate by the side of the house, and my hopes were raised: it seemed that indeed this young man lived there. He took the bicycle clips off his trousers and pushed his bicycle through the gate. I saw a flash of green grass and a small garden. He propped his bicycle against the wall, leaving

6

the side gate open, and went into the house through the back door.

I took a pair of opera glasses from my jacket pocket and focused them on the front door: number forty-four Adelaide Road. I powered up my mobile and typed the information into a people-finder account: the owner of the house was Mr Alexander Clearly.

Bingo, I thought, and then it got even better. I heard a window being pulled up and saw Alexander sticking his head out of the first floor window. He studied the people coming and going, just as I was now doing, and then sat down. He was still visible through the open window. Peering through the opera glasses, which I held in one hand so that I looked as if I was shielding my eyes from the weak sun, I could see that he was sitting at a desk and writing.

I stood and waited a while, thinking about the best observation post to watch him from. The front of Alexander's house was overlooked by other houses, but the best spot to station myself would be at the garage itself. I would have to try one of my usual ruses to gain access, and then spin out my story for a couple of weeks. Meanwhile, Alexander had disappeared from view. When he came back, he had a white envelope in his hand from which he took out a sheet of white paper. He read this – I assumed it was a letter – and then let it fall from his grip. He waved his hands about and uttered a few shouts of annoyance. I pressed the opera glasses to my eyes and saw his lips moving, but couldn't make out what he was saying. Then he disappeared from the window again. This time he didn't come back.

I took out my notebook and scribbled down my first observations of Alexander. He seemed lively, interesting, an open person. The side gate was still open; his bicycle was still leaning against the wall of the corridor between the houses. The first floor bedroom window was open to the warm air. With the right observation post this would be an easy job.

One hour later, I was watching Alexander from the garage across the road. I had been installed in the disused showroom, an empty room with grey plastic flooring and reflective windows that had once displayed the latest modern cars. The owner, a man called Mick, told me that he had lost the franchise and once the cars had been removed he had let the showroom stay empty. The windows had been treated so that people couldn't see in, a security measure intended to act as a deterrent against break-ins. I sat down on a wooden stool with my notebook and opera glasses at the ready. From here I could watch both the house and the comings and goings in the street. Mick had bought my story that I was an undercover policeman readily enough. It was a cover I had used on many other occasions. For a split second he had looked at me with a quizzical expression, and asked if we had met before, but I assured him we had not. His assistant, a Chinese woman with a name I didn't catch, obviously new to the area, brought me tea and biscuits. She bowed as she came through the connecting door from the garage shop.

So, here I was on the first day of a new job, settled down, catered for, and with the easiest brief I'd had in a long time. So far, Alexander had spent a lot of time upstairs in his house. He was in a room that had two windows, one large one guarded by wooden blinds, the other smaller and covered with dark blue plastic blinds. They had moved once, presumably when he'd brushed past them. I was to discover that the blue blinds were never opened. It didn't take me long to guess that they covered the window of his bedroom. The lighter wooden blinds were open, however, and I could see the vague shape of Alexander as he worked at his desk.

No doubt he was gazing out across the street, pen in hand, watching cars drive into the garage, observing the drivers get out, fill up, and pay Mick or the Chinese woman in the shop.

Alexander would also be watching the people go in and out of the Hay Wain. People-watching was his big interest, like mine, I realised, except that I wasn't a student artist. I watched him for an hour, finished my tea, and picked the biscuit crumbs off the plate. As I grew tired and yawned (one of the drawbacks of a sedentary job), he would be sure to do the same,. At least it would be lunch time soon: I quite fancied trying out the pub.

Any view of Alexander I might have had disappeared as Mick came into the showroom and crept up behind me. He asked about the case, who the suspect was, and if there were any developments. Mick was understandably agitated that one of his neighbours might be a source of trouble. I told him it wasn't like that at all; the suspect, whom I declined to name, was not believed to have committed any obvious crimes, no burglary or violence. Instead my task was to gather information; it was about how intelligence and knowing your suspect got you the results in the end, rather than any derring-do. The suspect, as I continually referred to Alexander, was on the fringes of a network that had been linked to white-collar crime, accountancy fraud and the like. HM Government might be a target, hence the state's interest. Mick was impressed, and obviously also relieved. He rubbed his messy beard and his messy hair and seemed to believe everything I said. He left me to it and I wrote a few pages in my notebook.

9

Just after I resumed watching the house the front door opened and Alexander stepped out. He'd obviously had enough of sitting down and wanted to stretch his legs. Now his face was lit by the midday sun it was clear that he was a good-looking young man, with a strong face and high cheek-bones and a full head of black hair. I could see why my client's daughter, and indeed other women, would be attracted to this man. It then occurred to me to check his marital status, which could be done easily enough when I was home and could log into the appropriate government website. I wrote 'check marital status' in my notebook. It would be unprofession-al of me to overlook pertinent details: for example, whether Alexander was already married, or even divorced.

Alexander was standing on the pavement outside his house. I took a photo of him on my mobile. I was at least forty or fifty feet away and handicapped by having to shoot through that dull blue reflective glass, but the photo would represent a start. He was waiting to cross the street. There were a few people walking past the garage on my side of the street who had also decided to stop and cross. There was a lull in the traffic, a break in the regular whoosh of cars, and everyone swapped sides quickly. Alexander stepped smartly across the road. Once on the garage forecourt, he turned to watch those who had crossed from the garage as they disappeared into the Post Office, which was just before the pub and a few doors down from his house. He scribbled in his notebook, and then loitered in the middle of the forecourt, watching the motorists standing at the pumps patiently filling up their cars. A couple of drivers, hard-looking men, gave him a mean look, but he stood on the edge of the forecourt and stared back at them. When the men had finished, replacing nozzles in holders, screwing on petrol caps, Alexander followed them. They were both tall with shaven heads and clad in black jackets. They all went into the shop.

I sat listening in the showroom, my head turned towards the connecting door to the shop, hoping to catch sight of Alexander up close. My heart was thundering in my chest. I was still thinking about the look on Alexander's face as he watched the motorists fill up their cars. He had been patiently observing them as if they were animal specimens. It was very odd: I wrote a couple of lines in my notebook, to record the oddness.

I got up and stood right outside the connecting door. I heard Mick serve a customer who was paying for petrol, two bottles of coke and a packet of crisps. There was no internal window to allow me to look into the shop. Another conversation started up, this time between Mick and another motorist, using virtually the same words: he'd bought the same amount of petrol and the same lunch. I continued to stand there quietly, waiting to hear Mick talk to Alexander, but I heard nothing. Eventually I returned to my seat.

Alexander was standing at the window, peering in, his face distorted by the reflective covering. I watched his eyes rove around, examining the room. For a moment he seemed to look straight through me. I held my breath, banking on the effectiveness of the reflective covering. Then he stepped away and turned his back to look out across the forecourt and the street beyond.

Alexander was talking as he stood there on the forecourt and watched the world go by. I could hear the words quite clearly. 'Oh, my people – stop! Forget your cars – refuel yourselves!'

I wrote this in quotes in my notebook as he also wrote something, scribbling furiously, bending down to balance his notebook on his thigh. I did not elaborate or speculate on the meaning of his words, I just gave the facts, as I was paid to do. I waited for more, but that was it. Alexander re-crossed the road, his head turning quickly from side to side as the cars rushed by, took out his key and was through the front door of his house in a flash.

It took a while for my heartbeat to slow down. I found something very exciting about this case. It was educating me, giving me different perspectives.

Mick knocked on the door and came in with another mug of coffee and a thick chocolate biscuit. He stood next to me and asked how it was going. I said it was going fine and thanked him for the refreshments. I didn't mention that Alexander had been standing on the forecourt outside the shop, where there was a stand for newspapers and charcoal bricks for barbecues, peering into the showroom through my window, or that he liked to watch Mick's customers. I didn't want to alarm Mick or make him suspect that Alexander might be planning a break-in, because then Mick might think about contacting the real police.

I commented to Mick that we, the unreal police, thought Alexander might be involved in something technical, computer hacking perhaps, something the young were known for. Mick's eyes widened, so I carried on developing the idea that Alexander might be part of a hacking collective, having watched a television programme about one the night before. Mick liked the idea, so I told him that if Alexander ever did come over the road to his garage, to the shop, for example, he should keep an eye out for the magazines or newspapers

Alexander was interested in. Mick was my eyes in the shop, I told him, and he loved that idea. Meanwhile, I would be watching for associates, the people who visited Alexander. Together, we would slowly but surely build up a picture of what he was up to. Mick went away intrigued and happy.

When I returned to the surveillance post I saw Alexander was once again staring out of his bedroom window: or, rather, he was staring at the inside of the window, looking at his own reflection. He had raised his hands and was running them down the glass, making the window blind, which had been rolled up to the top of the window, collapse and fall on to the desk. He stood up quickly; I could see him looking down at what must have been something interesting on his desk. Using the opera glasses, I could see that Alexander was smiling. The sun was on his face, and he was shaking with laughter.

I noted all this down in my notebook, in the entry for Tuesday. I suppose if any one of us were observed, secretly, throughout the day, and especially during the course of a whole week, we might also be the victims of slivers of time when we looked a little odd. So far, I had the impression that Alexander was inquisitive, fascinated by his surroundings and the people he encountered. He was also not shy of looking odd, or of appearing different. I was moving away from my original impressions of what he was like. He was young (how old exactly?), handsome (but did he know it?), and while he hadn't painted anything or made any sculptures while I'd been watching, I could see that he was soaking up the details of the external world as if storing them to provide divine inspiration.

I stood up and stretched up my hands towards the ceiling. I shook the life back into my legs. It was late afternoon, and the temperature was dropping, heralding the arrival of autumn.

I needed something to eat, something more substantial than tea and biscuits. I left the showroom by the back door, exited the garage from the rear, and walked out on to the side street where I had first observed Alexander riding his bicycle to his house. His bedroom window was still closed; there was no sign of him. I walked down the road, away from his house, and entered the Hay Wain. If Alexander had also decided to eat supper there, I would shrink into a dark corner, turn up my collar, and be at one with my pie and chips.

Nothing like that happened, although I did eat alone, with only a chicken and ham pie for company. I cleared my plate of the chips and peas and drained a diet coke. It was now six o'clock and time to knock off. The first day's report had been written. Alexander was an interesting mark. I was quite enjoying myself, and I thought more about the foreign holiday and where my wife might like to go.

Some regulars came into the pub as I was leaving. I stood outside on the corner and looked across the road at the garage. Mick was there, gathering up the unsold newspapers and taking them inside. I wondered what time he would close. The showroom reflected the image of the cars at the pumps. The window covering was effective; no-one could see in from outside.

A young woman rode up to Alexander's house on a bicycle. She was standing up on the pedals, a red light shining at the rear of the bike and a white light shining at the front. I stepped back into the shadows of the pub doorway and waited. She dismounted, walked up the front steps and knocked on the kitchen window, where a light was shining. Something caught her attention on the wall outside the house, and she picked up whatever it was, then disappeared through the open side gate, wheeling her bicycle beside her. I heard a door open. The young woman said hello, then came the smack of a kiss.

I stood for a few minutes waiting in the shadows of the Hay Wain. Was this woman my client's daughter? Was this Penny Travis? I described her in my notebook as five foot six, short brown hair, what appeared to be a fine figure under her jacket, and with a high, well-spoken voice as she greeted Alexander. Their relationship was now my concern. Penny's father was paying me to tell him what Alexander was like, and that included how he treated his daughter. Some fathers would do anything for their daughters, and that including hiring private investigators to spy on the young.

I walked up the road, away from the pub, past the post office, which was now closed, and approached the house. I stood back from the lit window in the downstairs kitchen of Alexander's house. I could see the kitchen sink and taps through the bottom of the partially open kitchen window. I stood behind two bins, one for the usual household waste, the other for recycling, and waited, watched and listened.

I could see two people moving in the kitchen: Penny and Alexander were dancing. A flush came to my cheeks as I felt embarrassed to be standing outside Alexander's house, peering in. I decided to walk on, further up the road, towards a corner with a street lamp that shone across the front of the house. I was aware that my having passed the house would have cast a shadow across the kitchen, and that anyone inside, whether sitting at the table eating, or standing at the stove cooking, or drinking beer and dancing, might notice a momentary dip in the light, look up, and perhaps even see me walking past.

But they didn't see me. Penny and Alexander were dancing to a Latino band. She was talking excitedly about what she had found outside on the wall of the house: a pair of opera glasses with a mother of pearl body and gold focus wheel. "Are you listening, Alexander?" she asked him. "You seem so distracted. What are you looking for? There's no one outside. Do you always have to be scribbling in your book?"

I heard Alexander apologise, and call her Pen, and there was the pop of a cork as they discussed who could have left the opera glasses there. I pricked up my ears when in hushed voices they agreed that it couldn't have been their neighbours, because they were drug dealers or suspected of being so. A more innocuous theory was that Little Red Riding Hood had been on her way to visit her grandmother, but the wolf had now made his move and it was too late to save her.

I understood where the partying was leading to and slipped away. I went the long way back to the river, where my car was parked off the road, on the grass. There was a Police Aware sign on the windscreen, which made me laugh. In my experience, the sign meant nothing, only that my registration number would have been taken and passed on to the council. I wasn't too concerned about it, so I removed the notice, thrust it into the glove box, and drove home.

CHAPTER 3

THE NEXT DAY was Wednesday. I knocked at the rear door of the garage and Mick let me in. He asked me if I had any news. I told him that it was still early days for investigation; Alexander might even be peripheral to the main action. Mick nodded and said he'd watched out for Alexander a bit himself last night. I was taken aback, but Mick said that he had still to clap eyes on the man. All he'd seen were vague shadows moving in the downstairs room of the house, the one next to the front door.

Mick then asked me what Alexander looked like. Did I have a picture? I didn't want Mick to get involved at all. Having a member of the public on the scene engaging in amateur surveillance would only spook Alexander, and potentially bring the case crashing to a close.

So I described an acquaintance of mine, one whom Mick would never meet: he's shorter than you, I said, thick neck, short hair, bit of a gut even at his age, and likes his fast food too much, bit of a slob, to tell you the truth. Completely harmless, but a wizard with computers, I added. With a man like that it was a case of softly, softly, catchee monkey.

Mick complimented me on my patience and professionalism. I said that it was just part of the job. No need to alert a suspect so close to his house; otherwise he would never feel comfortable and we would never get to see the real Alexander. Mick was pleased with this logic and promised to keep out of my hair. He had other things going on. With some coaxing and a lot of beard scratching and hair pulling, he told me that he was thinking of selling up. He had received an expression of interest in the site from a property developer who was keen to build more houses in the street. Mick had to be away a lot this week to negotiate a price and a date for completion, if indeed he did decide to sell. I could see that it would be a wrench for him to leave the garage. He seemed to appreciate my support. Five minutes later, Ying (I had finally discovered the Chinese woman's name) brought in a steaming cup of coffee and a slice of Victoria sponge.

The day burst into life just as my previous days at the garage had, with cars and people appearing and the noise and fumes increasing until by lunchtime I was glad to go out and leave that hot little hiding place. There had been no movement at Alexander's house, save for the postman parking his bicycle with the outsized panniers against the railings and shoving a couple of letters through Alexander's letter box. The blinds at both upstairs windows were closed. The curtains were drawn across the kitchen window. After all, it *was* a student house.

I went to the Hay Wain for lunch and ate the same meal as before, marvelling at the loyal and comfortable nature of pie and chips. I was three days into the job and I knew a little bit more about Alexander and his girlfriend Penny, my client's daughter. I wondered what they would be up to today and whether Alexander would leave the house so I could tail him, a part of the job I found thrilling.

A family came into the pub and sat down at the next table. Mum and Dad, son and daughter. The kids shared an enormous plate of fish and chips, Dad had the same pie as me, and Mum was brave and had a prawn cocktail. My wife missed me when I was working, as she worked mornings-only as an admin assistant at a local school. We had no children; they hadn't materialised, and after a while we had become comfortable with the situation. Deep down I knew that we'd missed out on a special part of life, but I also recognised that we'd been spared the difficulties that came with it.

I returned to the showroom via the side road and the back door, and, blow me, if another cup of coffee, and this time a plate of chocolate biscuits didn't appear in front of me, brought in by Ying, her hair in a new bob. Mick was away at his property development meeting. He was very sad, said Ying. I commiserated with her.

As soon as Ying had closed the door between the shop and the showroom, the side gate of number forty-four opened and Penny stepped out. She was dragging her bicycle along behind her. She had evidently spent the night at Alexander's, but the look on her face was not one of pleasure. Her white blouse was ruffled, her brown hair out of place. She had stuffed her jacket into an orange carrier bag, it being fairly warm today, and the bag was hanging awkwardly off the handlebars of her bicycle. She had trouble reversing the bike out of the side passage and while she was attempting this the chain came off. She let the bicycle fall to the ground, shouting her displeasure at the stupid machine. Alexander, who was standing at the open front door, also came in for some vitriol.

Penny's hands went up to her ears. She removed her earrings and handed them to him. As I watched Alexander, squinting through the showroom window without the aid of my opera-glasses, which I had lost somewhere, I thought he looked downcast. I lip-read the words, "Where have you been?" from her, and "sorry" from him. He tried to say more, but she cut him off and talked over him in her high tones. She then stepped over her fallen bicycle, knocked the notepad out of his hands, and marched back through the side gate. Alexander picked up the notepad. Still standing on his front doorstep, he started to write something.

The subject had a minor argument with the young lady at the side door of his property. The subject tried to appease the young lady, but the young lady was unconvinced by his efforts. I recorded these events in my notebook, dispassionately, as I had been trained, taking care not to speculate on cause or effect. It was a tiff between young lovers: wait until they tried marriage!

Then the light wooden blinds covering Alexander's bedroom window were raised, and the bottom part of the window was opened. Penny's hand appeared out of the window and something was thrown from it, an item which looked like a book. It landed with a thump in the small front garden of the house, just to the right of Alexander's doorstep. Then another item sailed out of the open window: a large pair of goggles, bigger than swimming goggles, silver discs in a black frame, more like welding glasses. There was a crack, as if something metal had been broken.

I slipped out of the showroom and through the rear door of the garage. Ying had been taking large plastic bottles of motor oil off the shelves and didn't see me. I dashed out to the side road and peered round the corner of garage. I wanted to be able to see and hear what was going on.

Penny's voice reached me from the window, her tone high and hectoring. The words were unintelligible but the sentiment was clear: she was not happy with Alexander, who had remained on the doorstep. She was annoyed about something he'd done or had allowed to happen.

The side gate swung open once more and Penny emerged, picked up her fallen bicycle, put the chain back on, and, disregarding the oil on her fingers, climbed on the bike, stood up on the pedals, and rode away. She turned right at the Hay Wain, and went off down the street towards the river, where I knew there was a bridge that would take her to the path to the city centre.

Alexander wrote in his journal for a while, and then turned his attention to the goggles that lay at his feet. He picked them up, turned them over carefully in his hands, and brushed the dirt off the silver discs and frame. He pressed part of the frame and frowned; I could see that it was bent and broken.

Alexander went over to his neighbour's house and searched a while for the book, peering into the space at the front of the house that was dominated by two wheelie bins. Two pedestrians passed by and noticed the young man searching in the undergrowth, and then writing something in a notepad, but they went on their way without accosting him. Eventually Alexander stood up, hands on hips. He seemed to have had a bright idea. He had not found his book, but he didn't seem to mind at all; he was smiling. He went back inside his house and closed the front door.

I waited for a while to make sure he didn't come out again. Then I crossed the road, skipping in front of one car and behind another, and stepped up onto the pavement. The blue door at forty-four was still closed. If she was watching Ying might think me mad, but I hoped she would be too engrossed in stock-taking. What if Alexander suddenly came out again? I decided that in that case I would just walk past, turning my head away, mobile phone up to the side of my face.

I needed something of Alexander's in order to really get to know him; probably whatever it was his girlfriend had thought wise to throw out of a bedroom window.

I approached the neighbour's house, paused, and looked in the exact spot where I had seen the book fall between the two rubbish bins. Sure enough, it was there: wedged upright and pointing towards me. I slipped on a pair of white latex medical examination gloves (every snoop needs to keep a pair in his pocket). I extended my right hand through the railings and took the book. Placing it under my shirt, I returned to the garage.

Back in the building, I sneaked back into the showroom. Ying was indeed busy stock-taking in the shop. Restored to my stool, I looked out at the road. The cars were still busy, but Alexander's house was quiet. His bedroom window was again closed, the blinds again drawn. The window in front of his desk was open, however. Did the man ever go out, or did he spend all his time inside, thinking great thoughts, or painting something, or whatever he did as an artist?

Perhaps this book might offer a clue as to what made Alexander tick. There was a picture of a house on the cover, a good-looking two storey house, and, in the foreground, a pencil sketch of a young boy who was wearing a sailor's uniform. Two butterflies had been sketched at the top of the cover, one in bright colours. The title of the book was *Speak, Memory*. The author was Vladimir Nabokov. I began to turn the pages. *Speak, Memory: An Autobiography Revisited*. The contents page was brief: it read Foreword, Speak, Memory and then there was an Appendix and an Index. I ploughed through the Foreword, which I found tough going. The first page of Chapter One was even harder: there was a word, 'chrono-phobiac', that I had never before encountered. I decided to abandon the book in favour of continuing my watch on the house.

I waited for more action; but there was no movement at the open window, or at the front door, or the side gate, which was also still open. The windows of the house looked back at me blankly. He's making a point, I thought. He's had an argument with Penny and now he's angry, upset, and he might well sit inside all day, if he's of that frame of mind. I still clung to the hope that he might venture out. The open side gate looked very inviting; I had fantasies of nipping inside the house to see what it was like.

It was beginning to get cold in the showroom as the autumnal sun dropped lower in the sky. Despite the hot drinks and a microwaved sausage roll brought to me by Ying, I was hungry again. I wanted to avoid piling on the pounds because of this case. I yearned for Alexander to do something that would relieve my boredom.

It was six o'clock. Ying had cleared away the daily newspapers and was closing the garage. I made the last entry in my notebook and decided that I would also call it a day. Mr Travis hadn't actually asked for a dedicated stakeout, merely an overall sense of what Alexander was like, but I was well on my way to providing a very detailed report. So far Alexander and Penny, like many young lovers, if indeed they were lovers, had had an argument. A strange device, a pair of goggles of unknown function, had been thrown from the window by the young lady. She had also thrown out a book, an auto-biography by a writer called Nabokov. Generally speaking she didn't seem well disposed towards the young man at the moment.

I asked Ying about Mick and his meeting. No news, she said, it's all up in the air. I bid her goodnight and walked down the side street to the river and my car. There had been no further activity from the council.

The light was failing as I sat in the car and checked out the book by Nabokov. I took a deep breath, remembered my training (every detail is important) and read some of the frontispiece and Foreword. The book was indeed an autobiography, but one which had been revisited. Nabokov had revised and re-remembered, making me wonder how much was real and how much invented or supposed. Anyone in police work knows how poor the average person's observation skills are, how lousy most people's memories, how selective we all are with our facts. Here was a writer trying to figure out who he was, he later claimed. At least Nabokov was aware of the problems such a quest presented, and how unachievable was the ambition to be an objective observer. Everyone observes others, speculates and then thinks they know what a person is like, but in my experience it's only the surface we see. We barely know ourselves, let alone have the ability to understand another person. Throughout our lives we embrace great changes. If I were to think back to when I was a child or a young man, I would hardly recognise myself.

I refrained from writing such reflections in my report. My client would expect the plain laboratory report on Alexander, the bald truth made from observation alone.

One page greatly attracted my attention. It was when Nabokov described something he called 'coloured hearing.' When Nabokov spoke, or mentally formed the image of a word, in his mind the letters took on different colours. His entire alphabet seemed to be coloured. For instance, the English '*a*' had the tint of weathered wood, but the French '*a*' was different, like polished ebony. Alexander had evidently disagreed with Nabokov: in the margin he had insisted, in angry red pen, that '*a*' was the colour of straw-coloured cider.

I shook my head at this and looked again at the words on the page, barely visible in the evening gloom. I took a moment to close my eyes and imagine the letter '*a*'. It was a plain '*a*' and rhymed with hay. Perhaps that was why Alexander thought of straw?

I read on and learnt that Nabokov's '*g*' was 'vulcanised rubber' and '*r*' was 'a sooty rag being ripped'.

'Really?' I spoke the word out loud, sitting by the side of the river in the front seat of my car, in a quiet space away from the usual surge and fall of the traffic. You could rip a rag, but why did Nabokov insist on a sooty rag? Did he think that '*g*' was made of rubber because the letter sat on its tail and looked springy?

There was a full-page description of Nabokov's entire alphabet. It all sounded very fanciful to me, but not to Alexander, who had let rip with his red pen and scribbled his own interpretation of each of the letters of the alphabet, starting with his hay-sounding straw-coloured cider, and ending with a sharp '*z*' like the flash of a silver sword blade.

One passage had me laughing because it showed me that Nabokov was joking with and teasing the reader. He had written: 'Finally, among the reds, *b* has the tone called burnt sienna by painters, *m* is a fold of pink flannel, and today I have at last perfectly matched *v* with 'Rose Quartz' in Maerz and Paul's *Dictionary of Color*.'

I put the book down, tilted my head up to the roof of the car and laughed out loud. The sound was more a bark than a laugh, and a man and his dog walking on the towpath (he a balding blondie in a Barber, with the look of a barrister just beginning at the bar; the dog a standard issue black Labrador).

There were tears in my eyes, and when I wiped them away the tears streaked the back of the latex gloves. I took care not to get the pages of the book wet, as I would have to return it to Alexander. I wondered how many people took this stuff seriously. From the Foreword I learnt that Nabokov was a famous fellow. Well, perhaps I'm a simple fellow, a mere po-liceman, an ex-police officer to be exact, but this all looked very suspect.

'But *b* is for burnt,' I whispered, not wishing to make a scene. 'And *m* looks kind of like a fold of pink flannel!' But I couldn't even get my head around *v* and Rose Quartz.

The clincher that made me suspect that Nabokov was pulling the leg of his readers was the section in which he explained to his mother about his coloured alphabet. He was a child, playing with a set of coloured bricks, each brick a letter and a colour, and of course, the boy Nabokov told his mother that the bricks were the wrong colours.

'Rubbish!' I said, deliberately softly, aware of how exercised I was getting, and I cringed in my seat. I must have looked a bit odd, sitting in my car alone in the dusk, shouting at a book. I put it down to all the caffeine and snack food, and no chance to work them off. Being confined on a stake out would make even the most placid and patient observer go nuts, and I was heading that way. So this is what writers and artists get up to, I thought. Being a plain-thinking ex-copper, experienced and unimpressed by the fanciful thinking of those who consider themselves different and better than us, I had a simple term for this so called 'coloured hearing'. I called it 'making it up'.

As I flicked through more pages of Nabokov's book, Alexander's annotations became more interesting and revealing. At the end of one chapter, where there was a half-page of unused white space, he had written: 'Could this ever be useful for remembering facts? My colours are different, so they are not absolute. No Forms here; another dead end.'

And in brackets, in a blue pen, and smaller writing: 'Keep this quiet from P. Who would admit to hallucinations? The leaking of a synaesthete's mind is tedious. Am I schizoid? As strange as the birds in the garden? It is true: I tend to fly in all directions.'

I was quite struck by these last comments. Did Alexander think he had schizophrenia? I stopped to remember what I knew about the condition. Did he hear voices? Did he hallucinate? And then it hit me. Did he think someone was watching him? Was he paranoid?

I put the book down and looked out the car window, away across the river to the meadows that abutted the city centre. This was interesting: what if Alexander suspected that he was being watched? Did he even imagine that his girlfriend's father would arrange such a thing? One thing was certain: I must continue to work carefully and remain undiscovered. If my role were revealed, Alexander would be vindicated. I didn't know what he might do then.

I remembered the look on his face, pressed up against the showroom window, as he stood inches away from me, eyes searching for something inside, and uttered those strange words: 'Oh, my people – stop! Forget your cars – refuel yourselves!'

He sounded like a priest in a pulpit, someone to be listened to. Give up these modern ways, these modern contraptions, cars and petrol and fumes and pollution – and accidents, I might have added: I'd seen enough of those. Slow down, stop, refuel yourselves. What was the fuel? A priest would have said God, or the Holy Spirit, but what did Alexander mean?

More to the point, what would my client, Penny's father, make of all this, if I wrote it in my report? Would the suggestion that Alexander suspected he was schizophrenic raise a red flag? Would Mr Travis forbid Penny from seeing her handsome and interesting, yet possibly sick, boyfriend again?

I wasn't used to dealing with such sensitive personal information. When I was on the force I dealt with common oiks, people whom I'd grown up with in the school playground. Everyone develops a sense of whom you can safely play and hang out with, and equally understands others who are just simmering with trouble. Years later I would nick some of them: petty thieves, arsonists, drug dealers. But it was the road accidents that wore me down. I finally left the force after one too many. I've seen enough death and misery on the roads to last more than a lifetime. I took early retirement, and became a private eye, at first specialising in tracing missing persons, but with a patchy success record. Then I changed tack to updating rich clients on the status of family or business members; and then graduated to undercover investigations. The job requires patient observation and a large serving of nous. There are no books to advise you on how to do it, and I admit that it's still an unexplored world for me. My wife would laugh if she saw me sitting here at seven o'clock in the evening, reading a book. Let's face it, I dodged any specialist police or forensic work because of the all the bloody forms and books. But, like every copper, I've got a PhD in people. I know and understand people. I can read them better than any book, and I can tell when they're lying, properly lying, not just having a laugh, and I can tell when they've got something to hide. I know when they're bent, not just a little bit wild, but properly wrong. Despite all this wealth of experience, I couldn't quite work Alexander out. Was he serious? Was he mocking himself? Or did he really have an undiagnosed mental illness?

The last page of the book was interesting. On the facing page, the flyleaf I suppose you'd call it, Alexander had written a neat paragraph in careful blue script: 'God is to be approached through the imagination, as a kind of art form, a symbol that expresses the mystery, beauty and value of life. The mystics understood this through their use of music, dancing, poetry, fiction, stories, painting, sculptures and architecture; they knew that these were all ways to express the reality that goes beyond concepts.'

Then in a looser, more flowing style, no letter allowed to trail too far below the line, Alexander had written: 'Is synaesthesia the way? Is this the way for me? Was it the way for Nabokov, Kandinsky, Messiaen, Scriabin? If I become a synaesthete, could God then communicate with me? Would I in turn be able to communicate God to everyone else?'

I snapped the book closed. The sharp sound resonated like a gunshot in the confined space of the car. They say you never really know what a person is like, but in this instance my quarry had helpfully written down the contents of his head. The book was an extremely useful insight into Alexander's character, and I had come by it quite legitimately. After all, I had not stolen it; I had merely picked it up near his house.

It contained nothing about Penny apart from the line about

keeping his gift hidden from her. What was his gift? He could read and write and speculate and imagine, but there must be more to him than that. What was the grand project Penny's father had mentioned? What went on in Alexander's house seemed impenetrable and, like all incomprehensible things, quite fascinating.

Something else intrigued me about Alexander: he was very into himself. He saw himself as special. I wondered if Alexander ever got rough with his girlfriend. He didn't look the type, but you never know. It's said the quiet ones are the most dangerous.

It was now properly dark. My wife would wonder where I was, though she hadn't texted me yet. I started up the car, admiring the smooth rumble of the engine. To know what Alexander was really like, I would have to get into his house. I knew I'd have to be patient and wait until the opportunity presented itself.

CHAPTER 4

T HE NEXT DAY, Thursday, I tried taking a new approach to the case. I had spent too much time at the garage; I was sick of biscuits, and also afraid that Mick, or Ying, would decide to start watching Alexander. I parked the car in the same spot by the river, certain now that the council was not interested in me, and walked away from Alexander's house. I knew that if Mick or Ying did get lucky and actually spot Alexander they would only be too delighted to report what they had seen to me.

I needed to do some research. If Alexander really was a student, I would have to find out where he studied. The city lacked a cathedral, but it had a university of some repute, a second university that when mentioned in the same sentence was snorted at, and several further education and specialist colleges. I squeezed sideways through the bike barriers and headed across the bridge towards the city centre. The bridge rose high above the river, and was of a modern design, long enough to have viewing areas, and wide enough to have dual bike and pedestrian lanes. The bridge bounced a little as I crossed it. On the other side, it joined a road next to the river, which I followed, walking towards a wide expanse of grass beyond which lay the city centre. The boat crews were out, young men and women in twos or fours or eights practising by rowing up and down the water, diminutive coxswains at the sterns calling out the strokes. I passed underneath a mighty concrete bridge and kept on walking until I reached a large meadow. The boat club was busy with men and women, all wearing all-in-one body suits, either launching boats into the water or lifting them out.

I passed some enormous cows, hulks of black and white flesh, huge necks stretching down to the green grass. Young people on bicycles passed me, silently creeping up behind and then zooming past in a rush of air and the chime of a tardy bell. A girl was sitting on the grass reading a book, the folds of her blue dress arranged around her in a square so that the book appeared to rest on her lap as if it were a table. She was a pretty girl, and the more I looked at her, the more she mesmerised me. I became quite captivated by her. She had long brown hair which she wore in a plait over one shoulder, and a crown of red flowers rested on her head. One arm was propped up on her knee. She held her hand to her face as she read, her other hand pinning down the pages as they were stirred by the breeze. Her dress was open at the breast, revealing a white camisole. I managed to tear my eyes away from her as she looked up so that she would not see me staring at her so blatantly. Still I noticed that her feet were bare.

A group of musicians was approaching her carrying guitars and drums, which helped me to make sense of the scene. I deduced from the conversation I overheard as I passed that she was the singer of a folk band.

I carried on across the busy ring road and went down a street where there were music shops and several pubs. I was walking on cobblestones now and realised that I had reached the edge of the city centre. I pushed on through the surging crowd. Colleges and churches towered above me. At length

I found myself in the market square and took a seat at a café on one corner of it.

A gentleman was just leaving the café as I approached and I had slipped into the seat he had vacated, jumping the queue. I ordered an espresso. The waiter brought it to the table in a proper white cup and saucer. I asked him to bring me a newspaper, too. I put on my sunglasses and sat and sipped my espresso, watching people come and go in the busy street.

People-watching is very much part of my line of work and there is no substitute for practice. I noticed that some of the people patronising the café were principally there to be seen: for example, the woman with her two daughters sitting at the furthest table. They were all dressed in white and wore black sunglasses and gold necklaces. Some men seated at the counter of a nearby coffee shop were appreciating the display, and the women were obviously gratified. In the middle distance, at the heart of the market, two kids were hovering around a sweet stall. I could see they were waiting for the stall-holder to turn his back so they could pilfer sweets undetected.

I suspected the middle-aged man at the second-hand book stall – he might have been an academic, judging from his brown shoes and flapping trousers – who was piling books up high on the wobbly, wooden trellis table was fighting with a similar urge to slip a couple into his brown briefcase.

The café was now full. My espresso burst hot and sweet upon my lips. I was enjoying soaking up the weak autumn sun and trying to get into Alexander's world. I was still reading the news on page one, each story in order, never skipping or missing anything, when I noticed a hush, a sudden absence of the chatter and noise of the crowd, as a young woman appeared. My hand jerked involuntarily and the espresso ended up in my lap. I made a manful attempt not to squeal as I used the newspaper to hide the stain on my trousers, my nuts burning with pain.

The young woman immediately became the main focus of attention of everyone in the café. Everyone sat up straight; one or two people even stood in wonder, as we regarded this beautiful woman. She seemed to give us a reflected pride in the nobility of the human race.

The waiter dragged out an extra table and set down a chair for her. I had seen this woman before, but only through opera glasses. She was my client's daughter, Alexander's girlfriend, Penny Travis.

She showed no signs of anguish following her argument with Alexander. I wondered, however, at her ability to withstand the stares of the crowd. The mother and daughters trio behind me were agape, their mouths little 'o's. I was embarrassed by my wet crotch, even though I had covered it with the newspaper, but still fascinated by the effect she had on everyone. I scanned her face again and again. What was I looking for?

She was wearing a white summer dress split to reveal a golden thigh. A red headscarf had been wound loosely around her neck and over her shoulders. She carried a black purse. Her expression was disarming, her eyes an extraordinary iridescent blue. They were peacock's eyes, eyes that mesmerised, drew you in, tempted you, but ultimately pushed you away, intimidated by the perfection they represented.

Shortly afterwards she was joined by two friends. They were both young women, almost as beautiful as she, but dressed in loud clashing colours. Their presence broke the spell. Slowly, the chatter in the cafe started up again, and the noise of the market grew louder. I was convinced that all the women sitting at the neighbouring tables wanted to rush to her side and become her devoted ladies-in-waiting.

I would have liked to stay longer but now I knew myself to be truly invisible, my presence wholly unnecessary, and I realised I could leave without embarrassment. I tossed some change on to the table and walked off, my folded newspaper still held firmly in place in front of my soaking trousers.

It was a long walk back through the city centre and over the river until I could again reach my car, and drive home. I decided it was too far to go in my present state, so I stopped at a department store, selected a pair of trousers in a shade of beige that matched my jacket well enough, and put them on in the changing-room. I thought I looked good in the mirror; encouraged by my appearance, I also bought a white shirt to complement the outfit.

I felt a great deal of empathy for my client. Obviously he recognised that his daughter was possessed of a rare beauty. Of course he needed to know what Alexander was like. I castigated myself for not having done more to help him. While it was true I was still only working in the first week of the case, I felt I had made little headway. I knew little about Alexander's intentions: in fact, I had not even met him properly, or seen him close to. I felt I knew Penny much better: she was passionate; she argued; she fought; got cross; spoke her mind; and suffered no fools. The display she'd put on at the café was akin to that of one of Nabokov's butterflies, sitting with wings exposed on a flower in the garden. Here I am, fellas: come and get me!

I sat down on a low wall at the edge of the market. The morning sky was brightening as I turned over these thoughts.

My client needed to know what sort of man Alexander was because he realised that there were men who would be capable of anything were they to lose such a woman. How might Alexander react if he lost Penny? I shuffled about, getting comfortable in my new trousers. Had Penny ridden away on her bicycle for the last time?

I came back to my earlier question: what exactly did Alexander do all day long? What was his big project? I spent the rest of the day doing more research.

CHAPTER 5

I T WAS FRIDAY. I was back at my observation post early. Mick brought me in a bacon sandwich made with proper doorsteps of white bread, the two rashers dripping tomato ketchup, and a hot cup of coffee. He really was a very generous man and reminded me in many ways of my father. I declined his offer of milk in the coffee; I needed the kick of the caffeine.

'You're young to be a detective,' commented Mick.

'Yeah, I took a few exams, made detective constable early on.' I stroked my beard, which had grown fuller overnight, just to make the point that I wasn't that young. 'I'll be thirty later in the year,' I added.

Mick nodded. 'I've never seen anyone in that house. Which one is it again?'

I pointed out Alexander's house, the blue front door, the blue side gate. The windows with the blinds habitually closed.

'He's being very careful, then.' Mick took a swig out of his cup. 'Must be on his computer all day long, getting up to no good.'

'From what we know of these hacker types, they start work in the evening and carry on into the small hours, then sleep in the day. It's classic anti-social behaviour.'

'Then why do you come here during the day?'

Mick had made a good point. 'Just being thorough; we've another team on him in the evening.'

'Really?' Mick's reddened eyes widened underneath his

messy hair. He rubbed his face as if he was trying to wake up. 'Where do they hang out?'

'I can't tell you that, but I can assure you it's not here. Of course we wouldn't expect to put anyone on your property at night without your permission. We have several strings to our bow.' I gave him what I hoped was a penetrating look. 'I'd appreciate it if you kept that information under your hat.'

Mick nodded. 'Anything to help our boys in blue.'

True to my prediction, the morning passed by without any sign of activity at Alexander's house. Just for a moment, I thought I saw him at his desk writing, but then the sun ducked behind a cloud and I was left unsure. I spent the time completing my first week's report to my client. In plain, workmanlike prose I wrote what I had seen Alexander do and whom he had met. When I mentioned Penny I gave her name, described her as a young woman in her mid-twenties, and gave an account of her meeting with Alexander outside the house and how she had gone inside. I described the little scene they'd created the next day, the argument, the returned earrings, the two objects thrown from the window. I wrote from an objective viewpoint, as I had been taught. I was merely a camera that reflected, in the pictures my words conveyed, how two people had interacted. I understood that Penny's father would very much like to know more about what his daughter was getting up to with this man, but I didn't have much more to tell at the moment. I had no further evidence, I could only speculate.

I finished writing in my notebook and snapped an elastic band around the cover to keep it closed. On the front I wrote *The Book of Alexander*. I pocketed it and stepped out from the back of the garage into a warm but muggy day. Ying was there, smoking a cigarette; she informed me that Mick was away at another planning meeting. I told her that he hadn't missed anything concerning the case. Like many student types, Alexander put the world to rights at night time when fewer people were watching. Ying called Alexander a lazy bum and we both laughed at that. We chatted for a few more minutes, then I said goodbye, and strolled off to the Hay Wain for lunch, as had become my custom.

One advantage of a steady routine is that it's easier to notice when something out of the ordinary occurs. If I'd toured the city's pubs, cafes or restaurants, perhaps in search of better food (it wouldn't have been hard to beat the fare offered by the Hay Wain), I'd have been distracted by new surroundings and different people. As it was, I had got to know the Hay Wain, and Nigel behind the bar, and become familiar with the menu. The first rule of surveillance is to be mindful of what's around you, focusing on each thing in turn; the second is to ensure that you make yourself blend into the surroundings.

After lunch I spent some time in the small post office, noting the top shelf of glamour magazines, as they're called now, the ice cream freezer, and the one-of-everything-on-the-shelves approach of the proprietor, an Indian man called Yash. I bought some chewing gum, which I believe keeps my teeth nice and white, and which also helped remove the cloying taste of chicken and mushroom pie and chips.

The afternoon passed uneventfully. It ended by offering nothing extra to add to my report. Even the drinks and re-freshments had ceased; Ying was obviously too busy. I went out into the shop and saw that half the shelves were bare, and that Ying was packing up the rest. Mick was still away. It dawned on me that soon I'd no longer be able to hide in the showroom to spy on Alexander. Ying was occupied with the final stock-take; she apologised and showed me where the kettle was, at the back of the shop. I made a cup of tea and finally managed to resist the biscuits.

I sat down in the showroom and gazed out over the fore-court. I honestly felt sorry for Alexander because he had un-wittingly been made the focus of such unwarranted attention. OK, he was dating someone's daughter: it wasn't a crime. Sometimes I wondered about my profession. I was spying on someone who had done nothing wrong, but I was more than happy to take the money for this. And I had had to lie to Mick and Ying, decent people whose way of earning an honest living was coming to an end. I hoped they would both be all right.

It was five o'clock and I was beginning to nod off, my notepad closed, when a taxi pulled up and waited outside Alexander's house. I ran out of the back entrance of the garage immediately, sprinted past the Hay Wain and headed down the road to the river, where I'd parked my car. My quick think-ing paid off. I was back in my car, parked on the corner near the pub, when I saw Alexander come out of the house, smartly dressed in jacket and trousers, and dive into the taxi. I took another gamble and followed the taxi, but not too closely, keeping at least one car between it and my own car. I could see that Alexander was the only passenger. I wondered why he was taking a cab when he owned a bicycle. Perhaps he really was lazy, as Ying had suggested.

I tailed the silver Hyundai, made conspicuous by its white rooftop taxi sign and hackney carriage plate on the boot. The taxi was weaving through the streets towards the city centre. It was cruising down the side of the central park when it stopped suddenly and Alexander stepped out. He was dressed in a blue jacket, white shirt, and beige trousers. He stepped smartly up to the door of a wine bar that cowered under the gaze of a Catholic church on the corner of the road. I continued driving until I'd reached the far side of the junction when I slowed down enough to see him standing inside the wine bar. He was in the act of greeting a young woman who was not Penny Travis with a kiss on both cheeks. I parked in the nearest free parking bay, placed a blue disabled badge on the dashboard and hurried back to the wine bar on foot.

I entered a softly-lit and warmly-scented place that was mainly being patronised by men in their fifties and women in their twenties. A blackboard on the wall advertised deals featuring trays of oysters and buckets of chilled champagne. Alexander was standing at the bar with his new girlfriend, ordering a shot of warm sake for him and a Virgin Mary for her. I stood next to him and ordered a pint of Guinness. The black and brown liquid was running slowly into the glass as I listened to their conversation.

'Is this part of your plan?' the new girl asked Alexander. 'Do you leave all your dates alone in a bar to get chatted up by middle-aged losers?'

'Sorry, I couldn't get away. Too much work on.' He waved his notepad, a gesture intended to include all the occupants of the bar. 'This will not be me in thirty years' time.'

'Really?' She laughed. 'The man devoted to a life of sensual pleasure? A man studying the mysteries of beauty? I know all about you, Alexander Clearly.'

'I'm sure you do. I'm a simple and straightforward man, Ruth, really I am.' He sipped his sake, letting the liquid roll around his tongue.

Ruth giggled at Alexander's words, and they touched

glasses with a clink. I moved away to a table in a darkened corner where I could sit and observe them unobserved myself. Ruth was wearing a sober office suit. She was standing with her feet a hip-width apart (hers were the girlish hips of a twelve-year-old, I noted) and kept gradually rising up on the balls of her feet, then holding the stretch for a few seconds before relaxing it. She repeated this routine often as their talk and laughter merged into the other merry goings-on in the bar.

When I had drained my pint I went up to the bar to order another one. It would have to be the last one of the evening unless I decided to order food and eat there. I particularly disliked eating evening meals alone in a public place; strange for a detective, maybe, but what else would make one look more like a detective, or a restaurant critic, or a middle-aged loser?

'What are *you* working on now?' Alexander asked Ruth. 'You should tell me: I've told you all my secrets.' 'Well, we're working on something for you-know-who, for fireworks night.'

'No, I don't know who. Tell me again.'

She pushed him on the shoulder, eyes twinkling, and earrings swaying. 'I know you think what I do is crap, but it's the way the world works. It's important to me, OK, so no laughing or I won't sleep with you.'

'OK, I'm not laughing.'

'Right, so it's bonfire night, and you take a sparkler, light it, and it burns in the shape of the star that hung over Christ's birthplace at Bethlehem.'

Alexander said nothing for a while. He was busy writing in his notepad. Then he pursed his lips and whistled instead of continuing the conversation. 'Gee whizz, who the heck thought of that?'

I had my back to him and was reading the menu, but it was unmistakeable that his tone had changed.

'We all did,' Ruth said in a small voice. 'It was a committee decision.'

'And what do you do when the sparkler's gone out?'

'These things can be made to sparkle a long time. Anyway, when it does eventually go out, the sparkler retains the star shape. Each one is patterned differently in gold, silver and bronze. It's quite expensive to get the effect, but it's meant to be representative of the three gifts from the wise men, and the idea is that everyone can bring their star to church at Christmas.'

Ruth paused to catch her breath. She evidently wanted to impress Alexander but the dynamics had changed between them. Alexander flicked his finger at the side of his shot glass.

'I see; sparklers with a special message. So, this is what happens when you graduate and go into public relations.'

He said it in a cheerful way and Ruth didn't seem to take offence. 'Come on, I got a two-two in anthropology. What else am I going to do? Anyway, Marston Fellowes pays well, and the boss likes me.'

The barman placed a round of drinks on the counter: cold sake and another Virgin Mary. Alexander waved away Ruth's efforts to reach for her purse and paid for the drinks with a large banknote. They chinked glasses and I felt even more of a gooseberry than I had before. I texted a quick message to help myself create an exit strategy.

'The real problem with it all,' she said, 'is what exactly the payoff is. Sparklers might be okay for bonfire night, but it's a once-in-a-year event. The take-home message is "go to church,", but that should be an all-year-round thing.'

43

'You could try: "Use it or lose it" – churches close every year.'

'That's better, something direct. But I was thinking of something much bigger, with more authority.'

'What did you have in mind? Co-opting a bishop?'

'No, hopeless, no-one listens to bishops.'

'A celebrity? Someone who's a Christian?'

Ruth shook her head.

'What, then?'

Ruth looked up to the ceiling.

'Good luck with that one,' Alexander laughed. He couldn't stop laughing. 'Hey, I can see the adverts now. You could be at a garage, filling up your car with petrol, and a voice would boom out over the forecourt: 'Remember, remember, the twenty-fifth of December.' The punter would look around and see no-one and then there would hear an echoing voice: 'Listen to the Man Upstairs'. And then I guess the tag line would be something like: 'Never seen, never heard, but probably there, at least maybe there.'

Alexander's laughter was infectious. I found myself grinning, but Ruth was not amused.

She was red-cheeked, not from the drink, but her embarrassment. 'It's not that bad an idea, is it?'

'Oh, no, it's a great opportunity. Like the wind in the trees.'

She looked at him. 'I like that! That's subtle, that could work.'

'Have it, please, it's yours. Tell your boss you thought of it.'

'Thank you, you're so clever.'

She leant over and gave him a kiss. I glanced across to see Ruth close her eyes as her lips met his. Then she took off her jacket. She relaxed her shoulders noticeably.

44

'Can we eat? I feel as if I'm just filling up on tomato juice.'
'Of course, let's order. Hey, partner, anything good on the menu?'

'Who are you talking to?' asked Ruth. 'And what on earth do you keep on writing?'

Alexander was evidently talking to me, but I was already escaping through the door, my head down, reading the new text message on my phone. I hoped Ruth might not have seen me.

I crossed the street and kept walking until I was well away from the wine bar. I headed down the road until I reached a bus shelter, from whose safety I could look back.

Alexander had a second lady friend, and a very pretty one at that. I would record the information in my weekly report, dispassionately, but accurately. Ruth would be described as a young professional woman, the word 'pretty' wouldn't be included. Mr Travis would read my words and sigh. The news would be welcome, not completely unexpected, and a good reason to warn Penny off Alexander. And to be fair if Alexander was capable of flitting around so easily, just like one of Nabokov's colourful butterflies, Mr Travis really was genuinely doing his daughter a kindness.

It would be odd for me to carry on waiting in the bus shelter ignoring all the buses that passed, resembling a pervert in a raincoat, collar up, face hidden. Alexander and Ruth looked settled for the evening; it would probably be another two or three hours before they emerged, no doubt holding on to one another, their cheeks touching. I truly would have taken on the role of the middle-aged loser if I had stayed to watch them kissing under the lamppost. I had to move on. There were plenty of CCTVs in the city centre; a man loitering at a bus shelter, his eye on the front door of a restaurant, would be bound to attract attention from the officers stationed in the civic control room. People have no idea the extent to which their movements are monitored in an urban area. I had myself sat in control rooms watching people do all sorts of things, amusing, alarming and disgusting. Watching someone from afar was undoubtedly the best way of finding out about them.

Alexander and Ruth had my good wishes. Perhaps when they came out of the wine bar they would head across the park, or over to the shopping centre, or go into the cinema for a late movie. Or perhaps they would carry on up the cobbled street to see if there was a more challenging film showing at the arts cinema. Some leaflets describing such films were blowing in the wind around the bus shelter. And whenever, and wherever, the evening ended for Alexander and Ruth (and I prayed Mick, or Ying, weren't camped out in the showroom, like vigilantes, determined to protect their empty shop and garage from the possible attentions of the man who lived across the road), I knew when I filed my report in the morning it would only contain the details I had gathered in the early part of the evening.

CHAPTER 6

THE NEXT MORNING, Saturday, I was back in the showroom. My cup of tea had hardly reached my lips when the first of many beautiful young women of that day turned up at Alexander's front door. Mick stood next to me, transfixed, as we watched the young woman, a blonde, arrive on a bicycle. It wasn't Penny; of that I was sure. She stepped off the machine lightly and rested it against the railings in front of the house, in the precise spot the postman had used. Then another two women walked up to the house. I saw a bus drawing away from the stop further down the road and guessed they had just got off it. Another woman arrived in a car that left again immediately, a man's hand waving goodbye out of the window.

These four young women stood outside Alexander's house, giggling. The first, the blonde with shoulder length hair, was wearing a blue beret, a short grey top that covered her neck but not much of her midriff, a blue denim skirt and white shoes. The two women who had arrived together were older; one was a silvery blonde with very long hair, dressed in a black jumpsuit. Her brunette friend was holding a phone to her ear, her other hand resting against her long hair as it lay against her neck. She was wearing a long-sleeved shirt in an abstract pattern, with pink cuffs. The fourth woman, the one who had arrived in the taxi, stood slightly apart from the others, dressed as if for an evening date, in a red gown with thin shoulder straps. She sported very large, leaf-shaped earrings. Her black hair was cut short at the back, but with a long fringe at the front.

'Bloody hell,' said Mick. 'Look at this lot.'

'He's a confident young man,' I agreed, stroking my beard as if it were a cat.

'And you said he's a computer hacker. More like a gigolo.' Mick was clearly envious. 'What I'd give to be young again.'

'It could be a front,' I said, 'but you're right, it's an unusual turn of events.'

The front door opened, and Ruth appeared, dressed in beige trousers too big for her and a voluminous white T-shirt. I had changed into jeans and a striped shirt for the weekend. She giggled and laughed with the girls.

'I've got to hear this,' said Mick, and he reached up and opened a long rectangular portal at the top of one of the windows. I had to stop myself from replying or making a grab for the window. Amateur! Did he want to give away our position and ruin everything?

The noise of the cars rushed in, but in a lull we heard Ruth say: 'Alexander will be back in a minute. He's just popped out for a few things.'

'So he does exist!' Mick turned to me in triumph.

'Of course,' I laughed. 'He's reclusive, but we have seen him about.' I felt a little cross with Mick, who must all this time have been putting me down as some sort of idiot, sitting here watching, if he actually believed there'd been no-one to watch.

Ruth waved the women into the house and closed the front door. I could see that the side gate was closed as well. I considered it poor wisdom to leave a bicycle unlocked outside the house, but at least we would see if anyone pinched it. Mick and I could see dark shapes in the kitchen, moving about, and then, a moment later, the four women appeared, two in each of Alexander's windows. The blinds had been raised, and the women were looking out and laughing. Then they turned round and sat on the windowsills; we watched their backs for a while. Finally, they all moved away from the windows, going deeper into the rooms. Ruth pulled down the bedroom blinds, leaving them moving in the slight breeze. We watched for a few more moments. My tea was cooling and I wished Mick would go away. Eventually Ying called to Mick, and he had to go back into the shop.

I recorded only the bare details of the women's arrival in my report. I noted down that the young blonde was about twenty, the other blonde in the black jumpsuit was in her mid-thirties and the older women were forty or more. Of course I had been some distance away from them, but my experience as a copper enabled me to gauge people's ages pretty accurately. In my report I called them 'guests of Alexander'. The reason for their visit became apparent later in the morning.

The young blonde appeared at the open window in the room where Alexander had his desk, exactly where I had seen him writing. Nothing happened in the part of the room that contained his bed; the dark blue blinds remained closed. The blonde woman was wearing the goggles that Penny had thrown out on to the street. She was patrolling the room as if searching for something, and then she waved her hands as if she could see herself waving her hands. She was moving about with her hands out in front of her, as if she was feeling her way and couldn't see properly because of the goggles. I eventually got the idea that she was watching some alternative reality through the goggles.

Ruth appeared next to her, now dressed in clothes that fit her rather than what must have been Alexander's white T-shirt. She was wearing a lilac T-shirt that moulded to her body. Ruth looked up and down the street, and then, for one long moment, across at the garage. I remained stock still until she retreated to the interior of the room again. Presumably she was waiting for Alexander to come back. I wondered how much trouble he would be in when he returned. I heard her laugh with the young blonde and I swear I heard the word "nervous", then both women disappeared from the window and I saw nothing more of any of them that morning.

What did these goggles do, I wondered? What could the subject see when she had these goggles on? The way in which the young blonde held up her hands while walking about suggested that she was watching herself from another viewpoint. If this was so, was she seeing herself truly for the first time?

I urgently wanted to find out the secret of the goggles, and I had a yet greater desire to understand Alexander properly. I was no longer content to sit there impassively and watch him conquer the women of the city. It wasn't enough to be plied with Mick's tea and biscuits or know that I would be picking up a load of money at the end of the case and taking the wife on holiday. I wanted to be able to write down in my report exactly what Alexander was like. Even though Penny was no longer part of the equation, and Mr Travis, my client, would no doubt relieved about this, I wanted to get under Alexander's skin.

Nothing more happened until lunchtime, when a taxi drew up and honked its horn. The front door opened and the four women came out of the house, tumbling together down the front steps, still laughing and smiling.

'Give our love to Alexander,' said the woman in the red dress.

'Shame he couldn't be here today,' said the brunette.

Ruth offered many apologies, the women kissed one another goodbye effusively, twice or three times on each cheek, and the taxi took them away, back towards the city centre. Ruth re-entered the house and closed the door.

A few moments later, just as I was leaving, the side gate opened and Alexander appeared. I saw that he was moving softly, pacing himself, and that he was careful not to let the gate bang as it closed shut against its wooden frame. He crept out to the front of the house. It was evident that he had avoided the four beautiful women by hiding in the garden, and that he was also avoiding Ruth. It was very strange: perhaps our Lothario had been overcome by an attack of nerves when faced with no fewer than five beauties?

Alexander took something from his back pocket. It looked like several squares of white paper, which he placed in the blue-lidded recycling dustbin. He paused a moment and wrote in his notepad, which evidently he took with him everywhere. Then he crept back down the side of the house, negotiated the gate without a sound, and disappeared back into the garden.

I walked over to the Hay Wain and sat down at my usual table. Nigel came over, placed the menu in front of me and asked me what took my fancy. I wanted something familiar, something that reminded me of home. A plate of steaming steak and kidney pie with chips and peas, covered in an extra layer of thick dark gravy, arrived ten minutes later. This was my favourite. Next Nigel brought me a pint of Guinness, all without saying a word, like a good barman. I ate slowly and thought about the case, chewing each mouthful thoughtfully. The report was going well; it could almost write itself, such was the interesting character of my mark. Of course, by now Penny would have informed her father about that cad Alexander and exactly what had gone on in their relationship. I wondered if I would hear from Mr Travis, or if he would stick to the plan, even if his daughter was now at home crying her eyes out, and he already knew the worst.

Alexander, it seemed, had no problem moving on. Immediately after Penny, there had been Ruth, and a day later, not one, but four, other women had appeared in his life. He might have lost his bottle – really who could take on five lovelies? – but I took my hat off to him for trying. He had changed much over the last few days, at least in my eyes, and I was growing to like this young man. At first I had thought him quite odd; I would never forget the sight of his face pressed up against the showroom window, and what he had said then. But his eccentricities now seemed quite appealing. Any man who could attract five beautiful women to his house must be considered special, even inspiring, and let's not forget the sixth, Penny, who was so strikingly good-looking that she had brought the market square to a standstill.

I wondered what actually went on in his rooms. Could it really be the obvious? And would I be reduced to spending the remainder of this assignment playing the part of a peeping Tom, watching Alexander conquer the local ladies, five at a time? I finished the pie and my pint, made a new entry in my notebook, and visited the Gents. On my return I paid up, thanked Nigel and went outside to smoke a cigarette. (I'd bought a new packet from Yash at the post office.) By the time I'd ground out the fag end under my shoe I'd decided I must find whatever it was Alexander had put into the blue recycling bin.

I walked along the pavement towards Alexander's house, conscious of how accustomed I had become to the area, how comfortable it felt. Mick or Ying might see me, of course, approaching the suspect's house, and would therefore know I was on the case. I wondered if Nigel and Yash knew Mick and Ying, if they were all part of a kind of shopkeepers' coterie. If so, what I was doing might have been spread around a bit. There he is, Mick might say, our young undercover police detective, working in broad daylight. No-one knew I was in fact a private dick working strictly for the money, and it didn't feel great to be deceiving them all. Still, no-one died, as they say in the movies.

I stopped just outside Alexander's house and listened. There was the sound of china being clinked in the sink: Ruth was probably washing up the visitors' tea cups. I would have to be quick, quiet and careful. I opened the blue lid of the recycling bin and peered inside. Five fragments of white paper were sitting neatly on top of the recycled contents. Holding the lid with one hand, I reached in with the other, took out the pieces of torn-up photograph, pocketed them and hurried away.

Once round the corner and back near the pub again I relaxed a little, crossed the road and headed towards the rear of the garage. Absorbed with piecing together the photograph, I nearly walked into a lamppost. I had to muster all my presence of mind neither to stumble into the road and fall nor stop dead still as if I'd been shot. I managed to keep walking, my eyes once again glued to the fragmented images which I held against each other so that I could get some idea of what the photograph had looked like when it was still intact. I entered through the rear door of the garage and nodded to Mick, who was standing forlornly in his empty shop clutching a clipboard. There was not an item left on the shelves.

Once returned to my stool in the showroom, I laid out the fragments on the windowsill and pieced together the picture. It was a photograph of Penny. She was topless and wearing long black evening gloves that reached her elbows. A white sheet was draped around her waist. A man's arm could be seen encircling her waist and holding the small of her back. The top of the man's head was visible inside a fold of the sheet. I couldn't read her expression. Was it one of ecstasy? Behind her was an old-fashioned white radiator, the sort that has thick elements. Above the radiator was a shelf on which had been placed a stack of books and a green teapot in the shape of an elephant. On the wall behind Penny was a painting of a tree. The wallpaper was unusual: it featured some kind of botanical pattern.

I heard the door open behind me as Mick walked in. I swept the pieces of the photo into my jacket pocket.

'Any clues?' he asked.

'How do you mean?'

'From today's bevy of beauties?' He stood by me and looked out of the window. 'I've been keeping an eye out, but I haven't seen anything else.'

'The women all left around about midday. It doesn't look like Alexander was at home, or at least he didn't show his face.'

'He's a funny one. I wouldn't be surprised if he's into a lot worse than computer hacking. You know: prostitution and the like.'

I blenched at Mick's idea. He saw the colour of my face change.

54

'Yeah, you get to hear a lot in this job, customers come in, crack on in front of you when you're serving them like you're not there. There were a lot of lovely women here today, got to be a reason for it.'

'You're an astute man,' I said, and I paused so that he knew I was about to divulge some valuable information. 'We know he's into high-end stuff, rich clients, bankers, hence the computer angle, and he also likes the finer things in life, nice hotels, yachts, and, yeah, women.'

'He's mixed up in all of that?'

I nodded, thinking quickly, not wishing to say too much. I knew if I did I would get out of my depth. 'It's the way of the world. Some say it makes the world go round.'

Mick shrugged. 'Perhaps I should get a job with him. I'm all done here.'

'I'm sorry to hear that.'

Mick stood in the showroom. He had already placed NOT IN USE signs on some of the pumps. He was a tall man and he stood up straight, trying not to look defeated. 'The deal's been done. I'll be all right, the company's been good enough to me, but I will miss this place. Ying's upset; she's only filling in, of course, but she really liked it.'

'Sorry, mate. You've been very welcoming. I'll mention you both in my report to my Super.'

He nodded. 'Demolition is slated for Monday next, but they need to seal the fuel tanks. I'm not open tomorrow.'

'I'll be done today.' Mick laughed. 'You'll have to get some proper binoculars if you want to keep up with him.

'Not those ancient opera glasses of yours. Where are they, anyway?'

'They're at home. I've got some proper German field glasses

on order.' I closed my notepad to make the point that I had finished. The title I'd given it, "*The Book of Alexander*", leapt out from the cover. I put my hand over it. 'Yeah, he's just a young man having his end away. I've concluded as much in my report.'

Mick left me to settle down for my final afternoon at the garage. When I was certain that Mick wasn't anywhere near me, I patched the torn photograph of Penny with sellotape. I debated with myself whether to describe this piece of evidence in my report. Would any father want to hear about, or see, such a picture of his daughter? I decided to say nothing about it.

Ruth came out of the house and walked away. She bothered neither with a bicycle nor with a taxi; she just slung her handbag over her shoulder and set off for the river, heading towards the bridge that led to the common and the city centre. I recorded her departure in my report. I was going to call her love interest #2 until I thought better of it, realising this was just speculation. She had looked business-like, her face set but registering no discernible emotion.

Alexander shortly appeared in the narrow passageway at the side of the house. He must have hidden in the garden all morning. He stood in the shadows, writing in his notepad, and then he disappeared again. When I saw him again he was sitting at his desk, the sun on his face, looking strangely happy like the cat that had got the cream. He was writing, his pen moving quickly. Occasionally he would look out of the window towards the garage and smile.

It was five o'clock. I was packing up and about to thank Mick and Ying for their hospitality and bid them farewell, when Alexander emerged from the side passageway wheeling his bicycle. He had a yellow clip around his right trouser leg. He locked the gate behind him, mounted the bike, and, standing up on the pedals, rode away into the dusk. There were no lights on his bike: I imagined that such mundane matters were simply too boring for him to worry about. I watched his voluminous white shirt billowing out behind him as he disappeared. By this time the garage was deserted. I called out my goodbyes to Mick and Ying, but the empty rooms reverberated with my voice alone. As usual, I left by the rear door, closing it behind me, walked down to the river, got into my car and drove home. Once I had parked on the paved driveway of our little suburban castle, I took one more look at the photograph I had repaired, then stowed it in the glove box along with Nabokov's book.

CHAPTER 7

THE NEXT MORNING I decided to work even though it was a Sunday, and I believe everyone needs their day of rest. Call me obsessed, but I liked the case I was on, and, even more important, I had a plan. I would gain entry to Alexander's house and find out more about him. I'd try especially to discover more about the project that Penny's father had mentioned, although that information apparently came to him second-hand from Penny.

It had struck me that the reason that Penny had been wearing the long black evening gloves was that when photographed on a black background her white upper arms would appear to stop at the elbows. This made her resemble a famous statue with broken arms. Its name was eluding me, so while my wife was catching up on the latest goings-on in her favourite soap I searched the Internet for details of an armless statue. I soon found the Venus de Milo, which confirmed in my own mind the point of Penny's get-up. I felt it helped me to understand Alexander better. What man with a girlfriend as beautiful as Penny could resist thinking of her as the goddess Venus?

I waited in my car for most of the morning, occasionally also wandering around near the river, crossing and re-crossing the bridge, until finally I had to leave. I couldn't be certain that Alexander hadn't returned home, but I had a hunch that he needed to get away. He'd let down Ruth, and he'd let down the other four women. How did he know they might not all turn up to confront him?

My wife had texted to ask where I was, and I'd replied I was in town hoping to pick up my new field glasses (they really were a lovely bit of kit and too good to be called binoculars); she just said be home for lunch. I didn't want to be disturbed again so I left my mobile phone in the glove box of my car.

I'd resolved to break in to his house. Let's be clear about this: I intended to force an illegal entry to his home. If I were discovered, I would claim that I'd found the front door unlocked and as a friendly neighbour I was letting the occupier know. Or perhaps I'd think up some other excuse.

As it happened, I gained entry to Alexander's house very easily; no-one was about to watch me. The garage was deserted. There was a sign in the shop window that said CLOSED and covers had been placed on the petrol pumps. The traffic along the road had ceased to a trickle. There was no-one outside Yash's post-office or Nigel's pub. It was a very dull, very British, Sunday morning. The apparently unseeing windows of the neighbouring houses might have concealed onlookers, but I thought that unlikely (and I was an expert in these matters).

Alexander's blue front door had a five-pin tumbler lock. I used a special set of keys to open it, a skill I'd learnt on the force. The fourth pin was the most difficult to manoeuvre into place, but then the others came together nicely and with one turn of the wrench the lock yielded, I opened the door, and then I was inside.

I had entered a wooden-floored kitchen. I shut the door and listened for five minutes, just standing there, taking in the noises from every part of the house. The fridge gurgled twice. Two cars passed outside, but after a short time I was confident no-one else was inside the house.

There was a large wooden table set in the middle of the kitchen. One tea cup stood on it, together with a note. "I guess you need some time but please call me soon. Ruth x. PS I want to be more than one of your experiments."

I wrote the content of the message in my notepad.

The white fridge was brightly decorated with magnets that held more scraps of paper. One recorded the address of a bank in the middle of the city centre; a name was also scrawled on it. A blue jacket, much like my own, hung from a stand near the fridge.

The draining-board was full of washed-up cups, mugs and plates. I remembered that when I'd stood outside I could hear Ruth washing up. She had held the fort and entertained Alexander's guests while he was goodness knows where. The kitchen was very clean and sparsely stocked. There was a kettle on the counter top with some packets of green and black tea standing next to it, but that was it. There was no toaster, no set of sharp knives, no spice rack and no fruit bowl. Not a lot of cooking went on in this kitchen. I wrote down these observations in my notebook.

The kitchen was open-plan and led into a sitting area where a green sofa and yellow chairs had been arranged in front of an open fire. The grate was clean, the coal scuttle full. There was kindling and logs left as if ready for winter, but when I peered more closely I saw there were cobwebs on the logs and a layer of dust. I wondered how long this pile of wood had been waiting to be burnt.

I turned from the fireplace to look out through the window into the small garden, which was mostly composed of long grass and wild flowers. I thought of the folk singer on the common. The garden was from another time, perhaps I meant Victorian; and very much what I would have expected of Alexander. I'd have been surprised if he'd built raised vegetable beds or maintained a bowling green. He seemed to be more sympathetic to unplanned nature and the beauty that comes from it.

The back door was concealed behind a large dark blue velvet curtain, useful, I supposed, for insulation during the winter. The garden path ran from the kitchen down to a grey, weather-beaten door set in the low brick wall that encircled the garden. There was a shed in the far corner of the garden, and I wondered if it was there that Alexander had hidden for hours on end. If he was quiet enough he could easily have come and gone from the garden, which led down to the river, without being seen. The path outside his garden gate joined the road where I usually parked. I noted this geographical aspect down in my report, but made it sound obvious, as if I'd known this fact from the first day and was just remarking on it again. I didn't want to be criticised for only adopting one vantage point. I needed to cover up that I'd neglected the back of the house.

In the furthest corner of the ground floor of the house, close by the foot of the stairs, was a solid-looking door. This door was heavy and opened slowly.

I walked into a room of bright light. Its walls shone white and were at first quite dazzling. In the middle of the room was a table with a projector and a laptop computer with its lid up, a cloud swirling on its screen. A microphone on a boom stand stood next to the computer. A video camera on a tripod had been set up by the table. Leads from all these devices were connected to the computer. The video camera and microphone were both aimed at the same spot on the white wall. A three-legged stool had been positioned under it. Next to the stool was a low wooden table bearing three bowls coloured red, white and blue.

I felt that I had got to the heart of the matter, to where Alexander really lived. I looked back towards the stairs, and listened again for any movement: nothing, not even the creaks of timber in the loft, always supposing it had a loft.

I was quite alone, so I relaxed and took the time to have a good look around the room. The laptop was idle, the screen saver working, the cloud whirling in and out. The video camera and microphone were poised, evidently ready to record the action of whoever sat on the stool. Closer inspection revealed that the lights on the video camera had been switched off; the microphone button was also set to the off position.

There was no reason not to sit down on the stool and look into the camera lens. The microphone was positioned a little higher and away from my head, waiting to capture my words if I spoke. Mutely, I shook my head. Through the window to my left I was surprised to catch sight of something colourful in the garden. It was a peacock strutting behind a fountain overgrown with tall grass. I sat motionless for a while, until I realised the peacock was really a statue brightly painted in iridescent blues and greens, the tail spread and the eyes looking up to the sky.

'So is this what artists do?' I said to myself, half expecting the video camera to stir or the microphone to wobble on its boom.

I was curious about the purpose of the bowls on the small table. I picked up the white one, which had been filled with a dark powder, and sniffed. The pungent aroma of vanilla assailed my nose. The red bowl contained small golden pearls that smelt of nothing. Taking my courage in both hands, I pressed a pearl against my tongue. Nothing happened, so I rested the pearl on my tongue and closed my mouth. Slowly, an oily sensation seeped into my mouth, followed by sweetness. The taste was delicious; I recognised it to be olive oil. Then I touched the velvet-covered legs of the stool and ran my fingers over the smooth fabric. It suddenly dawned on me what Alexander was attempting: vanilla, olive oil, sugar, velvet - smooth and delicious, exploring three of the senses. I looked at the video camera, smiled, and aimed a little grunt of pleasure at the microphone.

There was a click, and a whir, and the spinning of the hard disk as the laptop woke up. A red light blinked on the video camera. The projector on the table sprang into life and, slowly, the wall in front of me began to reveal a large square of projected light, the colour of faded parchment. The image of a dark-skinned woman with lustrous dark hair came into focus. I found myself smiling.

Music began to play: something sweet, with violins and gentle running melodies. The image of the woman disappeared. I was left alone with the music.

I got up and moved to the other side of the table to take a look at the laptop. It had recorded a video, which was now playing. First came images of the blank wall and the stool with the velvet-covered legs. Then I appeared in the frame. I sat down on the stool and peered into the camera with a questioning look. Several small white squares appeared over my face, computer-generated areas of focus centred on my eyes, nose and mouth. My cheekbones were highlighted. Then I turned my head and looked out into the garden, and the squares changed to rectangles, following my expression as I moved.

I watched myself on the screen, at the same time sniffing the vanilla, stroking the velvet legs of the stool, and allowing the olive oil to melt on my tongue. Then I lifted my head lifted and the white squares focused on my eyes, as I in turn focused on the face of the woman, and I smiled with pleasure. There was a strange noise in the background, like that of a satisfied animal. The music was playing: I cast around me for the speakers.

The video stopped and then the desktop screen appeared, the new video file highlighted. A folder on the desktop flashed. It was labelled 'Output'. I clicked on the folder and the printer slowly printed a colour copy of a face. It was my face, but only its contours were shown, with smoothed skin, cheekbones high and as if cut from glass, large eyes, small nose, and a large mouth. I had no hair in the computer-generated image, but this didn't detract from it. The face looked serene, happy, and peaceful. The image was of a minimal me, made during those few multi-sensory seconds when I had smelt the vanilla, tasted the sweet oil, felt the soft velvet, gazed upon the beautiful woman's face, let my heart strings be pulled by the string quartet.

It was a static image and I gazed at it for some time. There was a manila folder with 'Alexander Clearly' written on it in thick black pen. I put on a fresh pair of white latex gloves and picked up the folder. Inside were some legal-looking documents about the use of software. I replaced the folder, folded up my printed image and put it in my jacket pocket. It wouldn't do for Alexander to have such direct evidence of an intruder in his house, so I pressed the delete key on the laptop to remove the video file.

I left the room impressed with Alexander's art-generating device. I would have liked to stay to play with it, find out what happened when the subject was faced with other aromas and tactile sensations. I really was quite affected by the whole experience and had to sit down at the kitchen table for a while. No instructions on how to use the room had been left. All I'd done was turn up, and Alexander had worked his magic. Amazing that something so beautiful could be found in my old face. I've seen a few things, endured many others, so for a machine to find something wondrous in my features was amazing. Alexander rose much higher in my estimation. Yes, he did love himself a bit too much, but if he could show such creativity perhaps he deserved his self-esteem.

Outside the white room, at the foot of the stairs, was a photograph of a lake surrounded by trees. The trees were reflected in the lake. The whole scene was symmetrical, the edge of the lake providing a near-perfect horizontal line. Knowing that when Alexander was involved nothing was ever one-dimensional, I felt around the frame with my gloved fingers and discovered a small red button on the side of the frame. It triggered some music: a melody line on a rising oboe, another played by a dipping clarinet. The two melodies followed one another, just as my eyes followed the rise of the line of trees above the lake and the decline of the trees below the lake. A white card on the wall to the left of the photograph read: 'Lake Ekal. Alexander Clearly.' It was an interpretation of how a landscape might sound.

I went up a couple of flights of the stairs, treading carefully. The next photograph I found portrayed a mountainside. I found the red button on the frame and when I pressed it music played again: wintry strings that rose up over the peaks, and then grew deeper and more sonorous as the cellos celebrated the valleys. I laughed. This stuff could even be funny.

The stairs creaked as I went on, causing me to stop again. Alexander could easily be asleep in his bedroom. I looked at my watch: It was midday. He was known to be a night bird; I would have to get ready to run.

CHAPTER 8

I T WAS THE upstairs of the house that I was most interested in: Alexander's room at the front, in particular.
I couldn't turn back now, I was too deep into the case, so I
crept up the stairs to the top floor and stood on the landing
outside the bathroom. The door was slightly open, the yellow
tiles visible. I held my breath and listened. Nothing stirred,
nobody moved. I let my breath out slowly and thought about
my shoes. I'd made no marks on the wooden stairs. So far, I
felt I'd done a good job.

Past the bathroom I saw two closed doors and wondered
which to choose. The door on the left would give access to
a room that looked out to the back of the house. I knew the
door in front of me would lead into Alexander's room with
its two front-facing windows.

I tried the door on my left, but it was locked. I slowly let
the handle come back up without making a squeak. I wondered what the room might contain. The brown wooden door
offered no clues. I felt around the door frame, looking for a key
or a button, but nothing but dust came away on my gloves.
Maybe the room was just for storage? Looking up, I noticed
a small, square door set into the ceiling, the type of trapdoor
that might lead to a space under the roof for storing or hiding
away junk. I wished I could look through the closed door and
see inside the room, but I was prudent and didn't try to go in.

The door to Alexander's study and bedroom opened easily,

as I knew it would. Inside, it was more of a garden than a room, having trees and flowers printed on the wallpaper and a ceiling painted sky blue. The central lampshade was fashioned in the shape of a yellow sun. I recognised the fireplace from the photograph of Penny. It was now adorned with three china elephants of different sizes, painted in blue and gold and standing in a row. I knew that the other door, set between the windows, led into the bedroom, its dusty blinds never opened. I stopped and listened for a minute before I entered.

There was a digital frame by the side of the bed which depicted the blonde with the blue beret in a sequence of three photographs: one with the beret, two without, the last one as graphic as the ripped-up photograph of Penny. Alexander seemed to have moved on very quickly. After Penny, he'd spent mere hours with Ruth, who perhaps therefore did not warrant the capture of her image for his records.

Finally, I could relax: I knew without a shred of doubt that Alexander was out and I was alone in his house. I returned to the fireplace in what I will call the outer room and lifted the largest elephant off the mantelpiece. Its body began to change colour, from gold to red, so that I nearly dropped the damn thing as I felt it warm up in my hands. I put it back with the others and waited, alert for any other strange interactions.

I suddenly remembered seeing the blonde in the blue beret walking about cautiously with those strange goggles on. I looked up atthe corners of the room and spotted several cameras of the type normally used outside for home security. Four such cameras, white with black irises and pupils, were perched close to the ceiling, each near to an audio speaker. The best place to hide a camera is in plain sight, as people soon forget about them. These were high quality wireless cameras;

I suspected the images captured were relayed to the laptop in the white room.

I became aware of my image looking back at me from the mirror and thought of the taped-up photograph of Penny in the style of Venus de Milo. I stood back in the room in the approximate position where the camera would have been stationed. Perhaps this was Penny's role in Alexander's life? She was literally his muse, a goddess on a pedestal, simultaneously an example of living art. Perhaps this had caused some of their problems and their eventual split?

I performed a thorough visual search of the outer room, which I decided must function as a cross between a studio and a grotto. Alexander obviously liked to keep his house very neat and tidy. His writing desk was well-kept; he even had an old-fashioned blotter and inkwell. Curiously, it seemed to be filled with red ink.

The garage was visible through the wooden blinds. Red and white bollards with CLOSED signs fixed to them had been placed across both the entrance and exit. There were black covers on the pump handles. The shop had a large CLOSED sign on its window. The showroom's windows reflected the deadness of the site. I felt sorry for Mick and Ying, now evicted.

To the right of the desk were two bookshelves containing books of all sizes, some lying flat, others piled up in heaps. I scanned the titles on the spines: John Bowker's *The Sense of God*, Joseph Campbell's *The Hero with a Thousand Faces*, Sigmund Freud's *The Future of an Illusion*, Hans Kung's *Does God Exist?*, Spinoza's *Ethics*, Anthony Storr's *Feet of Clay*, Goulder's *Midrash and Lexicon in Matthew*, Karen Armstrong's *A History of God*. Wedged in the middle of this weighty stuff was a large notebook, much like mine.

I pulled the book out and read the title: *The Book of Alexander.* I sat down at the desk and opened it, laying it flat. The pages parted at the latest entry, which I saw had been made yesterday evening.

I cannot work today. My thoughts keep straying back to Melanie: her soft blonde hair, her scented body. I know nothing about her, but she seems to have flown into my net like one of Nabokov's pretty butterflies. I would stroke that butterfly if I could be sure that I would not damage it. I would stroke it, stretch it out, and run my hand over its contours. Mel-an-ee, my beautiful Mel-an-ee: pink flannel, chilli red, straw noodles, ebony, oatmeal, and finally the i of the bright sunshine yellow of the room in the Lenbachaus in Munich, where I made a pilgrimage to view the paintings by Kandinsky and others of the Blue Rider group. Overall, she shines with the golden colour of her halo, a most golden gossamer butterfly.

Captivated, I read another entry.

I am in a strange mood today. I do not need human company, not unless it is Melanie, but she is here with others. I close my eyes and see her halo, replaying the prick of my soul when the spike went in. I was the butterfly, not her, fixed to a cork board by a shiny gold pin, struggling under her desiring gaze. There was only one subject for me: Mel-an-ee: her lustrous hair, her slim body, her very berry lipstick, the softness of her cool cheeks. Mel-an-ee: the golden butterfly floats past my nose. Mel-an-ee: her touch, her eyes, her mouth, the lipstick, the sense of a per-fectly tanned body in butterscotch brown.

I turned the page.

And what of Penny? It is Sunday afternoon and I have not heard from her. I am not superman: I am normal, with normal

tastes, and I desire a normal relationship. But I am remarkable
as a neurological specimen, and it is a heavy cross to bear.

I let out a deep sigh as I read his more personal outpour-
ings. This was much more than my client needed. Clearly,
Alexander thought he was a special case, which was irritating.
But I felt protective towards him now that I'd broken into his
house and was reading his personal diary.

I turned the page again, going back in time until I found an
entry with a white letter stapled to the pages. The letter was
on headed paper, sent by a Dr Ling from a famous university.
The letter, originally neatly printed, was now bloodied with
red ink, presumably from Alexander's pen. He had crossed
out words and whole paragraphs in some places. He had in-
serted comments, sometimes in a scrawl I couldn't read, or
occasionally in very clear capitals using gnomic expressions
such as WHO KNOWS?

A journal entry had been started under the stapled letter.
It was the longest yet and took up more than two more pages
besides the one bearing the letter.

I am sick and tired of sceptical scientists, therapists and
doctors putting me through a battery of tests. I've had psychiat-
ric assessments since I was eight! And now they insist on blood
tests, or biochemical assessments, as they call them; I know it's
to check for drug use. The only drug I take is processed cheese
in a tube. They mock my intelligence by using the modified
form of the Wechsler adult intelligence scale: it tests junior
school vocabulary and a capacity for verbal similarities, picture
completion and block design. They think I am making it up,
Vladimir, they really do. They test my memory because they
think I make up and remember my descriptions so that there
really does seem to be a constant, coloured alphabet in front of

my eyes. *Seems to be!* Forget about seems to be, it is actually the case! I'm sure that my powers of recall and logical assimilation are advanced for my age, and perhaps I am eidetic; I experience visual images so vivid and sharp that they might as well be reality. But as well as being like reality, they actually *are* reality! I mean, isn't everything sensible a part of reality? I am not making this up! :-)

PS I do like the Farnsworth-Munsell 100 hue test. I'm quite sure that this test sparked my interest in abstract painting.

PPS I've stopped giving the scientists my most florid descriptions, aware that they were, just as my parents were, at first amazed, and are now, latterly, sceptical of the colours and lights I told them about when they played the piano together and the notes floated around the room.

Note to self 1: Do not mention to anyone what happens when you eat food.

Note to self 2: Whatever the doctors say, I do not have a mental disorder. How dull for them to want to classify everyone relative to the norm, which is only the usual and the boring. Their quest for normalcy just gives me a long row of golden 'z's streaming from my head as I wait for them to stop being so dull.

PPS Continued: WATCH OUT WORLD! I have sharpened my 'z's. Like Kant being awoken by Descartes, now z is the sharpest letter in my alphabet, big and bold, like the Z that Zorro slashes into an enemy soldier's tunic. Z is the slash of my intellect; it is the silvery metallic grey of surgical steel, the slice of a fresh scalpel blade, the physical counterpart of Occam's razor. It slices through a dull, lumpen argument like a scalpel cutting through a lump of lithium. It's bright and shiny and dangerous. A bit like me. LOL.

I flipped thought the rest of the journal, which contained

72

some more written entries but was mostly made up with photographs of unfamiliar people. It took me a while to realise that almost all these images had evidently been captured in this room. There were also a few examples of the minimally beautiful faces generated by the equipment in the white room.

Then there were sketches of Alexander's immediate surroundings: the street, the garage, the post office. I deciphered a diagram that revealed itself to be a birds-eye view of the area. It showed the house, the street that went up to the roundabout past the church and churchyard and down to the river, and the path over the bridge into the city centre. Going in the opposite direction, it showed the pub, then turned left to the main road, the way the taxis came and went.

The notepad had almost been filled. I assumed that was why it had been placed amongst the other books on the bookshelf. Inside the front page was a sticker, the sort that might be used in school books.

This book belongs to Alexander Clearly
(this is the Book of Alexander)
(excluded by the Council of Nicea).

It was a highly decorated book, which made it difficult for me to put it down. Alexander liked to decorate the corners of pages with quotations. '*Radical: to root out the truth, like a wind that threatens to lay everything bare.*' I thought back to the wine bar and his comment about the wind in the trees.

One of the last entries, scribbled in the corner of the same page as the sketch of the garage, proclaimed: '*Just because you're paranoid doesn't mean He's not watching you.*'

The word 'He' was circled, and a line ran from the circle to another paragraph scribbled in the margin: *God: the word conjures blackness, its spoken image driven hard by the initial* letter, G, *the blackness of space, but not a complete black, not quite a philosophical or physical void, a nothing. It is a slightly pliable, almost rubbery black that suggests that there is something tangible in the darkness. The ivory o and the walnut d are two brief flashes of light in the gloom: the bone and wood of Nature.*

Most disturbing, however, was the straight line drawn in pencil and with a ruler which ran from the front of his house to the showroom of the garage, along which a giant eye was drawn.

There was no time to read more: I could hear the sound of the side gate being opened and the clicking of a bicycle as it was wheeled through. I heard whistling and knew it must be Alexander. I took his journal off the shelf and hid it inside my jacket. I hurried down the stairs, the heels of my shoes slipping on the carpet.

I was out of the front door, closing it softly behind me, just as Alexander entered through the back door, having parked his bicycle in the garden. I was already walking towards the pub when I heard the side gate shut.

Alexander would be in his kitchen now. I'd left no trace of my break-in unless he spotted the most important thing of all: I had stolen his book. But the book was completed, so hopefully he wouldn't miss it for a while. If it was his practice to keep a journal I assumed he would have another on the go. I was pleased to know that I'd be able to give my client some extracts from his journal in my report. I was less happy about the knowledge that eventually I would have to return it.

I passed the post office, turned right at the pub, and walked down to the river. When I reached my car, I turned back and realised I could see the low garden wall at the back of

Alexander's house. I decided against moving the car. The fake resident permit was still good and I doubted there was much activity from traffic wardens on Sundays. I had been parking in the same place day after day, so that the weeds seem to be growing round the car.

I walked over the bridge, the river flowing underneath me. I was soon back on the common, the cows grazing there silently. I had turned up the collar of my jacket as a half-hearted attempt at disguise. Alexander's book weighed heavy against my heart.

CHAPTER 9

A s I'd worked at the weekend, the next day didn't feel like the start of another week. Another Monday, the second of this case! I drove in to work, leaving the car in the same spot, and then spent an enjoyable morning in the ancient city centre wandering around the old buildings. I had a good lunch in a de-consecrated church that served excellent vegetarian food, taking the opportunity to re-read some of Alexander's fascinating book. After an equally enjoyable and lazy stroll around some of the less well-known lanes and alleys, I returned to my car and drove home just in time to see my wife leaving for her book group. We're like ships in the night who never meet, I thought, as we kissed hello and goodbye. I went inside to work on my report.

On the kitchen table was an unwelcome letter from my client, Mr Travis. I found it annoying that my client had sent me a letter before he'd read my report, but I calmed my frustrations by focusing on the fee. My wife had already tumbled to the fact that I'd landed a big earner and had left several travel brochures about trips to Florida scattered about in the living-room. I wasn't about to let her down.

My client wrote that he thanked me for my work and was sure that I was doing a good job. He understood that Alexander was a popular young man, but that was of no concern to him now. He was no longer interested in knowing more about Alexander's relationship with Penny because he understood that it was over. He remained, however, very interested in Alexander's well-being, and admitted that he had concerns about Alexander's mental equilibrium. He wanted to know my views on this aspect of the case.

Towards the end of the letter he surprised me by making a confession. He apologised for having perpetrated a piece of subterfuge. He had originally signed his name as Anthony Travis and had made himself known to me as Penny's father; it now appeared that this wasn't true. To reinforce this point, and with a line drawn with a pencil and a ruler, he had crossed out the name 'Travis'. My client now signed his name Joseph Clearly, explaining his true status by writing below it (Alexander's grandfather).

I was, quite frankly, stunned at this duplicity. Alexander had switched from being someone of interest to his girlfriend Penny's father to being a subject of concern to his own grandfather. Was there no limit to how people could use the excuse of familial instinct, ostensibly to protect children, to spy on them?

Of course, I instantly doubted that I was now working for Mr Clearly Senior, as well as realising that I had never worked for Mr Travis. This indeed was a most remarkable case: I felt my chain being yanked. It probably says something less than honourable about me if I admit that again my thoughts turned to money. The focus of the case, Alexander, remained the same, despite the change of client identity; and what was important for a jobbing PI was simply to get paid. How else does one remain objective? The agreement had been for payment by bank transfer of a large sum of money on receipt of my report. Joseph Clearly, if that was who my client really was (I had a hunch that ultimately I would discover Penny behind this caper) had added a postscript describing how the payment would be made. The address of the bank was the one recorded on the sheet of paper stuck to Alexander's fridge. I was surprised at the coincidence that both men had chosen the same bank. Then I turned over the letter and saw that the route I should take to the bank had been specified for me. I once had a colleague whose client had done the same thing with the purpose of watching the PI in action, a sort of "watcher watching the watcher" scenario.

I decided to carry on writing my report. I was already in the second week of the case and reluctant to give it up. Whoever 'Mr Travis' really was, he had signed my terms and conditions, a legally binding document. I could if necessary chase him through the courts to recover my fee. That knowledge comforted me for the rest of the day.

CHAPTER 10

DESPITE THE YELLOW tape and the Keep Out signs, it was easy enough to open the door at the back of the garage. The shop was totally bereft, ready to be smashed down: even the kettle had gone. I sat in the showroom feeling a little nostalgic, even though I'd only worked there a short while. My gaze fell on that very familiar house across the street. I'm a simple fellow, as my wife will tell you, a horse who will work hard for a carrot. Now I'd allowed myself to become part of Alexander's clever little art project. The watching eye across the street, the objective observer who would tell you exactly what you were like, stripped bare of images and masks and pretensions. Many people would pay for such a service.

The blue front door opened and out stepped Alexander, dressed in a blue frock coat, buff leather waistcoat and breeches. He glanced up and down the road, even though there was no traffic, and then crossed over to the garage. He scribbled something in his notebook. Then a surprise, someone else followed him out: a middle-aged man, his hair flecked grey in places, dressed as a Victorian school master. They looked like actors in a play.

They sauntered around the forecourt as if it was a film set and stopped in front of the showroom window, behind which I was sitting, still hidden from them by the reflecting glass.

Alexander took a few steps forward and touched the 'Keep

Closed' sign hanging on the wall. He and his friend peered inside the showroom. I stared back and held my breath.

'Who do you think is in there?' asked Alexander's companion.

'The conductor, on a pedestal, stands in front of an orchestra.'

Alexander pressed his face up to the glass, as he'd done on the previous occasion. His milky white eyes roved around the room.

'Why do you think that? Do you have evidence?' asked the schoolmaster.

'I have no evidence. I just wish it to be so.'

His companion smiled and clapped him on the back.

'Write it all down. You're making good progress.' He hitched his trousers up around his narrow waist and snapped his braces. 'This is quite an itchy costume.'

'Thank you for your help.' Alexander stepped back. Then, suddenly, he leapt forward again, and shouted 'Hey!'

I flinched, wondering if he really could see inside the showroom.

'Can you hear what they're singing?' Alexander put his ear to the glass. 'If there was a conductor he'd wave his baton and trace the words in the air, written with multi-coloured fire.'

'Alexander, let's take this gently.' His companion took him by the elbow and tried to lead him away. 'There's no point upsetting or embarrassing yourself. You've said how much that affects you.'

'But look, why are they being kept out?' Alexander held on to the man's arm, jerking his head up and down wildly, pointing to the cars slowing, some half turning in at the entrance before driving away again, their owners staring at the oddly dressed men. Alexander staggered and his companion put out his arm to stop him falling over. 'Why can't they just stop and look and listen?'

'Well, they would do that if there was anyone here, but this place is deserted; it's closed.' His companion held him steady. 'They'll have to fill up somewhere else.' The man smiled and the lines around his eyes crinkled as he held on to Alexander, who was becoming progressively weaker, legs buckling, back bending. He fumbled for his pen as it fell to the ground. It was odd to watch such a tall, handsome man crumble into such a weakling. Alexander heaved himself backwards and leant against the window, his back only a few inches from my face. 'I know you're in there,' he said.

Then he fell silent and motionless. It was the first time I had seen him stop moving; he looked defeated. His companion stood over him protectively. 'Rest a moment. Do you want a drink?'

Alexander had a vacant look. He seemed lost and strangely subdued. Then the moment passed and he straightened himself up, got to his feet and with one hand pushed his weight away from the showroom window. He appeared to be completely revived. 'Why can't they just stop and listen to the beautiful music and then mankind will join together in wonderful harmony? The orchestra will follow the conductor's instructions and see-saw their ink-pens across their violins, and words will then appear in front of them on the pages of their books. I think there should be helpers patrolling the orchestra to take away the books when they are full. They should give them new books to write in, or old books to edit.' Alexander turned to his companion, who was wringing his hands and looking around nervously. 'Tell me, Young Werther, why?'

'I think I've indulged you long enough, Alexander. Didn't you say you were meeting Melanie later?'

At the mention of her name Alexander stretched to his full height. 'Forgive me. A man wholly under the influence of his passions has lost his ability to think rationally and is regarded as intoxicated or insane.'

His companion nodded. 'And we wouldn't want that, would we. Let's go back to the house so I can get out of this clobber.'

'I think I'll keep mine on. Melanie's bound to dig this, especially the beard.'

They walked back across the forecourt, crossed the road and disappeared into the house.

I was dripping with sweat by the time they left: it was peculiarly unnerving to be spotted in my fish-bowl and not be able to move or to escape. Why was Alexander dressed like that? Who did he think he was, and who was the other man? I got up and paced around the showroom. I seized a broom that leant against the wall and swept some dirt to one side. No doubt Alexander wanted me to write something flattering about his latest get-up in my report. I could hear my wife's voice as she encouraged me to flatter his ego and claim the rest of the money.

It was as if Alexander was an actor and wanted a good review on his first night. I replaced the broom against the wall, sat down and opened my notebook. I didn't feel like pleasing my client with a record of the latest scenario he had concocted, partly because I could not be sure who my client was. Was Alexander's grandfather really looking out for his grandson's welfare? Alexander was thirty; allowing about thirty years per generation, that would make his grandfather ninety. It was possible, but unlikely.

I sighed. All I could do was keep my report completely objective and write down only what I had observed. I would record that he liked to dress up and that he looked dashing as an eighteenth-century European gentleman. Why he did this, I would not speculate. I would, however, venture that his companion was there to help him, and was possibly some sort of therapist or doctor; and that they were engaged in what could have been a type of therapeutic play-acting.

The trouble was that if I wrote all that down Alexander would probably work out where I was watching from, and that wasn't on at all. I really didn't like that idea. As it was, Alexander's fevered imagination had attached too much significance to the garage, believing that there was a giant eyeball watching him from inside the showroom. For him to find me there, writing in a journal the way his musicians wrote music into books, could really have blown his mind. I couldn't afford to be found out. It would leave me without a vestige of professional self-respect.

But my wife's voice intruded and visions of Floridan beaches swam across my vision. The money at the end of this increasingly thin and make-believe rainbow was still very good. I shook my head. Someone wanted to know about Alexander's mental health badly enough to hire a private detective; and here I was, writing descriptions of Alexander at work and play. I wondered if I could track his therapist down and ask him if he liked the idea of flattering Alexander in his professional capacity, any more than I did in mine. It seemed that Alexander's ego needed rubbing every day.

Ah, to hell with it. I was this far in. The report was coming along well. All I needed to do was write a few pages of flattery and then I could take myself and the wife off for a very nice holiday. The first cocktail on the beach, I'd praise Alexander to the heights.

The front door opened and out stepped Alexander's friend, free of his itchy costume. He had changed into a tweed jacket and country trousers. He carried a slim briefcase, which convinced me even more that he was a therapist. Doctor, or Mister, or whoever, was whisked away in a taxi. Always the same company, I noted: six fives; Alexander probably had an account. I could tap up the taxi firm if I needed any more information on his acquaintances. When his therapist had left Alexander emerged, still dressed as an eighteenth-century German gentleman. He stood on his doorstep looking at the garage for a while, writing in his journal.

If he comes over here again, I thought, I will leg it out of the back of the garage and escape down the main road. He'd never catch me. I decided to chuck the stool out the back and sweep along the windowsill with the broom, just to remove any incriminating breadcrumbs.

But Alexander didn't come back. Very slowly he started to walk away from his house, past the post office and the Hay Wain and down to the river. He dawdled where the main road joined the side street and for a moment I wondered if knew all about me and wanted me to follow him.

CHAPTER 11

ALEXANDER MIGHT AS well have clicked his fingers or thrown me a bone: two minutes later I was trailing him at a discreet distance, far enough away that if he turned round I could change direction to ensure we would not meet.

We crossed the bouncy bridge and he picked up speed, stepping out at a fair pace across the common. I was quite a way behind him but he was easy to track. He attracted a fair amount of attention from fellow walkers, but no hostility. He could have been an actor in one of the Shakespearean plays held in the old buildings over the summer, although his arrival would have been a bit late for that. We crossed the ring road and I tailed him down one of the many side streets until he stopped outside a church. I waited patiently at a good distance, again like a faithful dog. Eventually the young blonde woman appeared wearing the same blue beret: Melanie, the blonde in the photograph on his bedside table. She laughed when she saw his outfit. Then they embraced, kissing on the lips, and she rubbed her face in his beard until it tickled her. They went inside holding hands.

There was a shop with an awning next to the church, Starlight Books, a Christian bookshop. I ducked into the archway and heard noises from the room above, which was beyond an old winding wooden staircase. There was an aroma of smouldering sandalwood. I met two young girls, aged perhaps between sixteen and eighteen, at the foot of the stairs.

'Hi,' I said.

'Hi,' they said, in unison. 'Are you here to let Jesus into your heart?'

'Yeah, for sure.'

The girls escorted me up the stairs. In a niche on the wall was a thin brown incense stick burning in a wooden holder. The sound of voices grew louder as we climbed higher, reaching the third and then the fourth floors. We came to a kind of tower room. Outside it stood a bouncer dressed in a black suit, mirror shades over his eyes, his head a solid, shiny bullet that pointed upwards from a bull's neck. He nodded to the girls and clicked his fingers. Two more girls, one white, one black, descended the stairs to take the places of the first two.

I entered the room, which was murky and muggy, made gloomy by heavy curtains of red and purple that had been closed. It was lit by a few candles. A two-bar gas fire was glowing red in the corner. Smoke drifted up from the four corners of the room: its scent was woody and musky. Music burbled from small speakers connected to a CD player standing on one of the window sills. There were about a dozen other people in the room, all seated on the floor, mostly cross-legged, swaying to the music, some with hands in the air, others with eyes closed, a few singing softly. Alexander and Melanie were to my left as I came in. He was scribbling away in his journal and she was trying to read what he was writing. I kept my face hidden from them, having turned up my coat collar. I kept my hat on.

It was hot in the room, but I was resolved to keep on my coat and remain undiscovered. All the newcomers were welcomed, the older hands pulling us into their group and draping their arms over us, placing their hands on our heads in

86

welcome. Soon the newcomers were also swaying along, trying to pick up the lyrics. When I had taken in what the songs were about I found them embarrassing. 'You put a tongue in my mouth and I want to sing to you.' 'Take me as I am.' 'Jesus, when I feel the touch of your hand upon my life. . . .'

I watched Alexander and Melanie. They were right in the thick of a group of fawning devotees.

Melanie, who had taken off her coat and jumper and un-buttoned the top few buttons of her blouse, was singing along merrily while fanning her face and chest with her hand. She held hands with those on either side of her, the blonde ringlets around her ears dancing under the dark of her beret. Soon I found myself singing along too. I was officially here to observe Alexander, but I knew I'd already stepped out of line a bit and now I felt he was leading me astray. It dawned on me suddenly that he was trying to reel me in. I didn't like the idea at all.

New songs were introduced, embracing more spiritual concepts: the lyrics called on the Lord to light the way, to direct our lives, to speak to us. The atmosphere in the room had changed. People called out, or yelled, and endorsed the songs by making strange sounds in their throats, rather than articulating proper words. People now swayed together as a single being with a common purpose. I felt the air wafting around me as people frantically waved their hands even though most remained sitting on the floor. Others tried to stand and promptly fell down: weightless and giddy, they dropped like heavy sacks to the floor, after a time springing up again, rejuvenated.

I wasn't very impressed with these young people. Like Nabokov, I thought they were guilty of making it up. Maybe their church had stagnated, and the working of the Holy Spirit had not truly reached their hearts. They had to find their own way and this was the best they could do.

A young woman next to me began stroking my arm. I saw she was one of the girls who had escorted me upstairs. I wondered if she knew what she was doing. Now she was stroking my leg.

She was pretty, why stop her? There was such a feeling of love in the room; it burst upon me that it was a pleasure to find after my adult lifetime of dealing with people who were obstreperous and dishonest.

The crowd began to speak as one in a language I had never heard before, if indeed it was a language. The woman in front of me burst into tears, then kissed me on the head, and then burst into tears again.

Some of the worshippers were calling out 'Yes!' and then 'No!' It was getting out of hand. I've been in crowds that suddenly turned into surging mobs and experienced panic when there was nowhere to run to. I saw Alexander get up, grab Melanie's hand and try to pull her upright. The crowd moaned louder, pack animals about to lose two of their number to predators. I stood up and the girl who had been stroking my leg also got up and tried to stop me leaving, still preaching at me in her nonsense tongue. I pushed her gently out of the way and bolted for the door.

'Let's go,' Alexander said to Melanie.

'Why?' Melanie was sweating and the lids of her eyes were half-closed. She lolled and tilted in his arms, barely in control of her actions.

'This is wrong. These people are trying too hard. Worse, they're fooling themselves. What they're saying is complete garbage.'

Alexander had managed to pull Melanie to the door when the bouncer blocked his way.

'She's ill. She needs some air,' said Alexander.

'No, I'm not,' said Melanie. 'I'm not ill. I'm filled with the Holy Spirit.'

The bouncer stared at both of them. I rolled my eyes; a faint smile played across his face. He shrugged and let us all past. I was happy to find he was prepared to be reasonable about it. No doubt tomorrow night he would be on duty outside a local nightclub or a pub, this was just his Sunday night's gig.

He let us leave and I headed down the stairs, leaving Alexander behind me struggling with Melanie. She was fighting him fiercely, so that at each step they took he had slowly to negotiate the next.

A voice shouted down the stairs. 'You're not leaving, are you, Mr Clearly? Why are you running away?'

Alexander struggled on with Melanie, who seemed drunk or intoxicated with some drug.

The voice called out again. 'What are you leaving behind, Mr Clearly, if there's nothing here for you?'

Alexander left Melanie slumped on the stairs and ran up them again. I took them two at a time myself, to catch Melanie before she tipped forwards and fell. Her body nestled into mine; I breathed in her perfume as we half walked, half slipped down the staircase. She put her arms around my neck, mistaking me for him. By the time we had reached the courtyard and the refreshing night air I was as giddy as she was. She peeled off me when we got outside and lay down on the cold cobble stones, laughing and panting.

'Are you OK?' I asked her, checking the doorway for my first glimpse of Alexander. I needed somewhere to hide.

She giggled and nodded her head.

'Are you drunk?'

'Drunk on love.'

'With your man.'

She nodded again, then sat up. 'Who are you?' she asked, but I was already on my way.

Alexander had come tumbling down the stairs, followed by a middle-aged man in a suit. 'But what troubled you tonight, Mr Clearly? Please take the time to explain it to me. Did someone suggest some evidence against your theory?'

The middle-aged man was tall, thick set, with a balding head and a goatee beard. He stood in the street like a wrestler prepared to fight, ready to take Alexander on. But Alexander wasn't interested in physical action. Instead he stood, head jutting forward, ready for a war of words.

When I look back on the case, this is the scene I remember most. In the next few seconds it became so surreal that it was as if I was an actor and had stepped into the wrong play.

Alexander took from his coat pocket a long bushy beard and a fake moustache and stuck them on his face, the beard extending outwards from his own genuinely bearded chin in a wedge four or five inches long. Already looking the part in his blue frock coat and buff leather waistcoat and breeches, he began talking with a heavy German accent as he addressed the assembled crowd.

'Here, tonight, I was looking for the original universal and Godly proto-language, the one to which I personally am attuned.'

The crowd fell silent.

'Instead, I witnessed incoherence; I did not see any correlation with the truth.'

There was a light ripple of laughter; his wrestler protagonist stepped forward, smiling. 'Who are you tonight, Mr Clearly?'

Alexander looked at him closely and reached for his beard. He moved back into the crowd. His interlocutor did not pursue him.

Melanie was watching quietly from where she was still sitting on the ground. She had rested her back against a bench and still looked pretty in her beret. Everyone who had been in the room above the bookshop was now outside, the sizeable group of people having filed out into the street and surrounded the two men.

'That,' said Alexander, waving his arm upstairs to where the crowd had originally been assembled, 'was all gibberish. My coloured alphabet is a far stricter construction than the gobbledegook that I heard up there, pouring out from so many empty vessels.' He began to pace up and down. 'None of the letters or syllables or phonemes was of a consistent colour, even when they came from the same person, let alone shared. Where were the semantics, syntax or morphology of the language?' He turned to the crowd. 'How could you possibly have been speaking the language of the Holy Spirit, or anything that could be called a language at all?'

He had balls, my client, I'd give him that, but at this moment in time he didn't have a friend in the world. It was as if he'd been at a pub lock-in and had then criticised the punters for getting drunk on the beer. I remained concealed behind a tree, debating whether I would go to Alexander's aid if things turned ugly. He was my paymaster, after all.

His goateed opponent spoke up, as clear as a bell: he was an obvious favourite with the crowd. 'Then why are you here tonight? Or maybe that's obvious.' He turned to look at Melanie.

The crowd wolf-whistled and Melanie dropped her eyes to the ground. This was territory more familiar to me: pub chucking-out time, when there was often a bit of banter on the pavement, and likely some aggravation to come.

Someone took a picture of Alexander on a mobile phone. My client didn't like that. He started to walk away, putting out his hand to Melanie, who did her best to stand up to follow him.

'Who does he think he is?' a voice in the crowd asked.

'He's a common or garden atheist, that's all.'

'Why the beard and the frock coat? Who is he?'

'He's Marx or Engels, that's who.'

Alexander had heard some of these comments and he halted, foolishly I thought. Melanie clearly wanted out of there, but he turned back.

'God and man are interlinked; they are the same. Man projects himself outwardly and looks at God in the mirror.'

'Speak plainly,' called another voice.

'Or shut up,' called another.

Alexander stood there, shaking, his hands balled up into fists. 'You believed he was revealed to you tonight. But you were wrong. All you did was to take a long look in the mirror.'

'So you're a proper theologian now, and not just an artist?' The goateed pugilist was enjoying himself.

'Theology,' retorted Alexander, 'the queen of the sciences. Study it no more, or you will see that everything man says about God has been invented to appease some weakness of human nature.'

'It's sad, isn't it, Mr Clearly, that you once came to us for

92

love and support, and now you have turned against us and poked us in the eye. We all have crises of faith. There are people who help you, but you have spurned them all.'

His opponent suddenly snapped his fingers and pointed at him. 'I get it now. You're Ludwig Feuerbach!'

Some of those in the crowd clapped their hands at this revelation. 'Trust good old Christos to work it out.'

'He's clearly gone mad,' said a voice, and the words were quickly taken up and chanted by the crowd.

I felt sorry for Alexander, standing there dressed up in a false beard and frock coat while the crowd showered him with abuse: 'Clearly, he's gone mad.'

'And now you invite women to your chambers and take photos of them and call it art.' The man called Christos was poking his face right into Alexander's. Not many blokes would have stood for it. Even the weakest man would have lost his temper and thrown a punch. Christos, if that was truly the man's name, was no hard nut; it might even have been a fair fight. But Alexander turned his head away, speaking quietly so that we all had to listen carefully to what he was saying.

'Yes, that's what I do. I have nature in my heart, powerful nature from which faint-hearted theologians hide.'

'Just call yourself an atheist and be done with it!' hissed Christos. 'And don't come around here no more.'

Christos went back inside the bookshop; most of the crowd followed him. I shrank away, hiding behind the corner of a house. Alexander rubbed and pulled at his beard and tore it off his face. Then he took off his coat, standing tall in his white shirt. He seemed unnaturally elongated; pale-faced with black hair, he resembled a matchstick.

Melanie grabbed hold of him and told him he'd been

incredibly brave. I had to concur. They kissed on the lips and I moved out of their line of vision, stepping down a stairwell that led to a basement. They walked past me, not heeding me, arms around one another.

'You were so brave to talk to them like that. How on earth can you write it all down at the same time? You're amazing.'

'Brave, foolish, it's all the same.'

'You're not foolish. You're lovely.'

He kissed her. 'Fancy seeing the late film at the arts cinema?'

They wandered off, the street lamps turning Alexander's hair yellow then orange as he passed.

CHAPTER 12

I WAS LATE to bed that night, so my wife was already asleep. I found I couldn't get to sleep myself until the sun was rising, when I finally nodded off. When I awoke, I found my wife had left a note on the kitchen table wishing me a good Tuesday. I sat at the table nursing a cup of tea, thinking about last night. What I had written in my report was stilted, procedural and didn't do the events justice at all. But then, I'm not a writer, I'm an ex-copper and a fairly inexperienced private eye. On the sofa that stood in front of the fire a couple of holiday brochures had been left casually open. I love my wife, but sometimes she can't half put on the pressure.

What I wrote should reflect how zany and entertaining a character Alexander could be, how amazingly attractive he was to women, and, on a more serious level, how he had something genuine to say to Christian types seeking revelation of God. I felt I was not equal to the task.

As I took a shower, it dawned on me why I'd been chosen to tackle this. I might be a lumpen tool, a dull pen with ink that didn't flow, but I was a trustworthy observer. I knew how to observe, I'd been trained by the best.

No doubt Alexander had many people to tell him he was either a wonderful or a crazy man. But what my client wanted was the truth, so he'd hired an expert to watch him and write it all down. I felt better as I towelled myself dry, but I knew that I still needed inspiration to match the challenge I'd been set.

I climbed into my car and drove down the main road, heading out of town to Alexander's house. I had opened the windows of the car to clear my head. I parked in my usual spot by the river. I still hadn't been rumbled: no one had discovered that the resident's permit on the windscreen was fake. I couldn't risk trying to install myself at the garage again, because it was now awaiting demolition. If he saw any movement inside, Alexander, who was obsessed with the place, would be sure to pluck up the courage to break in and discover me.

I therefore went to look for a spot where I could sit down and read, taking Alexander's journal with me. I didn't want to go to the Hay Wain as that would have invited too many questions from Nigel, the landlord. I could have gone home, but instead decided to walk out across the bridge and stop at one of the observation points. Any walker or runner passing by seeing a man reading a book on the bridge, legs dangling above the river, would simply have thought I was one of the studious types from the University.

I checked that Alexander wasn't anywhere about, and then I opened his journal and started reading it from the beginning.

'In the fading sun of a winter's afternoon, I sat at my desk and gazed across the fields towards the river. The land raised itself into a gentle slope and ran garnished parsley-fashion by the wood on the left, from where the fox was driven by the hunt, down to the far right corner, where the marauding horsemen got caught in the revenge of the boggy ground in the spring. Yesterday, the field was hard and dead. Yet, still, a lone bird, a large Canadian goose, had decided to land. It stretched its wings, packing them after its flight, and stood craning its long neck, proud of the space it had found for itself beyond the flock.*

I *commiserated with the goose, solitary despite the nature of its species, which was to be surrounded by others just like itself. In the distance the disturbed reflections of the sky indicated that there was activity at the river. Perhaps the goose would travel on there, I mused, but instead the goose turned and honked up at my window, its neck extending towards me like a black-tipped finger. Already on the slippery slope of reverie, the goose's call closed my eyelids and awoke the denizens of the dream.'*

What was this, I asked myself? When and where had he written this? I had noticed that Alexander didn't bother with dating his journal entries. He must have been out in the countryside when he compiled those words, perhaps standing in a field somewhere with a river nearby watching a hunt, the dogs chasing a fox. But that didn't account for the whereabouts of the goose, which he said had honked up at his window.

Where was this house situated in the middle of a field?

I read on, stomach gurgling, aware that during the past few weeks I'd grown accustomed to a friendly welcome by Mick or Ying, and a cup of coffee and a biscuit or two (I certainly didn't need them but I really enjoyed them). The next few lines revealed the answer to my question of the location of the watcher in Alexander's account.

'I *was a hunter, or a naturalist, waiting by an African watering hole, my face striped dark and light by the wooden blind of the window in the unknown house looking down on the unknown street.*'

Of course! He was in his own house, looking out across the street. And then, once he had retained me to work on his case, he had been looking straight out of his window at me, concealed though I thought I was in the garage showroom. I thought back to the day when the blind at his window had collapsed: his face had been striped dark and light then. The unknown house looking down on the unknown street was his house and the street was Adelaide Road. What was his point? What was he getting at?

I read on.

'No, perhaps I was a beetle-collector: in fact I was the student Darwin, peering intently at life in the ponds and rivers, watching to see what made them tick. Whoever I was, I maintained consciousness within the dream and watched the street life outside. The cars were too quick to focus on; they tugged my eyes from side to side and reddened them when I tried. I don't like cars, don't have one; can't even drive. I have a spectator viewing my thoughts, I think we all do, and the spectator labelled the cars as pikes and made them responsible for the danger in this hot, foaming river. In respite, the bicycles, the Queen's swans, slid silently and slowly by. I love swans, except maybe that black one from next door, whose dry brakes made it honk like a goose. Gleefully, I propelled the film onwards.'

I put the book down and looked out over the river. The street, his street, was a normal street. While the garage had been trading there had been a fair amount of traffic, but now the road was noticeably quieter. Adelaide Road was mundane in character, humdrum people and vehicles travelling both ways along it. Today's weather was grey but not wet, the air mildly warm. It was a typical autumnal day, offering fleeting memories of summer even though it was the last week of October. But nothing was normal for Alexander; nothing he wrote was boring, it was all pregnant with great meaning.

I read again about the cars in the river. That was OK, I could get that. He had made the bicycles into swans, gliding by, and that wasn't too much of a stretch. And I liked how the squawking sound of brakes on a bicycle could be the noise of a goose, supposedly the same goose that'd looked up to his window. There was a lot going on in his head, and now, after knowing him for a bit, I could make more sense of his writing through the lens of his own imagination. He was watching life in a hot foaming river – the street outside his window – from his ordinary suburban house. A lot of it was fanciful, but there was more to it than that; it contained self-control as well. Alexander knew what he was doing; he was self-aware. He was able to direct his dream, if what he'd written was a dream, and propel it along.

There was one line that really worried me. It was buried in the middle of the entry and very matter-of-fact. '*I have a spectator viewing my thoughts, I think we all do.*' He had asked his diary if he was schizophrenic, and I wondered if he could be or had once been, even for a short time.

The mention of someone else, some other, an outsider, seeing Alexander's thoughts reminded me of a criminal I'd nicked years ago. He was a small, goblin-like man with the most intense blue eyes and a habit of throwing himself at the walls of his cell, bashing himself up, shouting for us to silence the voices in his head so he could sleep. We called in a psychiatrist, who had only spent five minutes with him before he diagnosed schizophrenia. Then when the man woke up he told one of my colleagues that he was ashamed of what he had done – it was only burglary – but he might as well admit everything because he knew we could see his thoughts.

A man was standing on the bridge behind me. I heard the scuff of his shoe on the boards and kept my eyes fixed on the journal. I willed him to keep on walking until he had passed me. What would I do if it was Alexander and he realised that

I was sitting out here reading his journal, an item of property I had stolen from his house? But then I relaxed. This was such a crazy case, the usual expectations of observer and suspect bent so much out of shape already, that a little light pilfering would hardly be condemned. Alexander might even be pleased. I turned my head to look at the man, prepared to break into a big smile if it turned out to be Alexander.

Mick was standing behind me dressed in a grey suit. He seemed shorter now he was outside and away from the garage. I closed the journal and placed my hands over the front cover.

Mick nodded at me and then said: 'You've shaved that beard off.'

I smiled and rubbed my chin. 'The wife didn't really like it so much.' I stood up and stretched my legs. 'How are you, Mick?'

'Yeah, I'm all right.' We could both hear ominous noises coming from the garage, the sounds of heavy engines rumbling and the calls of several men. Mick looked towards the road; the garage was hidden from view by the backs of the houses. 'It's the final day of work. They've sealed up all the tanks and the demolition boys are in.'

'Sorry, mate.'

Mick shrugged. 'What you reading?'

'My son's English homework; he likes to write stories.'

'I didn't know you had a son?'

'Yeah, we've just the one kid. He's sixteen, a bit arty, likes to make things up.'

There was a great roar, followed by the sound of breaking glass. Mick's eyes were fixed on a spot beyond the houses, the place where his beloved garage was being knocked down. 'There she goes,' he said quietly.

'Any new opportunities for you?' I asked. 'Will a phoenix rise from the ashes?'

'Maybe. Company's got a site up north that needs a manager. Bit far for me, but beggars can't be choosers.'

There were further sounds of destruction and I felt Mick's pain as the garage was obliterated. I, too, would miss the place. 'I'd like to thank you and Ying for the hospitality, sorry that I didn't get a chance to say goodbye before.' I extended my free hand and Mick shook it. 'I've been very well fed and watered.'

Mick took my hand and held it for a while, testing the firmness of my grip. 'What's the verdict on his highness?'

There was a slight chill coming off the river. I put Alexander's journal under my arm and blew into my hands. 'Nothing at all; he's not involved in anything. We think it's a case of mistaken identity.'

Mick looked at me and then away again, down the river. 'I never saw the fella, not even once. Ying says she didn't either, and she's got eyes like a hawk. You were the only one to get a good look at him.'

'And the night surveillance team, but that's how it goes sometimes.' There was a lot of rumbling and revving of engines and then an almighty crash in the distance. 'Everything comes to an end,' I said, not very helpfully.

Mick tucked his hands into his fleece. 'I can't go back that way again now it's gone.' He shook my hand and, smiling, he said: 'You're no copper. Yash reckons you live around here.' And then he walked across the bridge towards the city centre and that was the last I saw of him.

Mick was an astute man. My impersonation of a plain clothes undercover police officer had held out for a while, nearly the entire length of the case, but then I had been rumbled by the salt of the earth. There was a limit to what I could pull off, how many people I could fool: Mick, Ying, Nigel and Yash had all known I was interested in the young man at number forty-four. Fate had decreed that the garage be demolished and I was glad not to have to pretend to Mick any longer. But I was winning: I had a few days' more surveillance of Mr Alexander Cleary to carry out and then I would deposit the completed report at the bank and be free of his narcissism. I could collect my reward and take my wife on holiday to Florida. Mick could think what he liked about me while I was sunning myself and swimming with the dolphins.

CHAPTER 13

AFTER THE GARAGE had gone I had to find another observation post from which to watch Alexander. I realised that I'd already solved the problem. I would wait in my car, as police do in the movies, and stake out the rear of his house. The demolition works had closed the road at the front of his house; now residents had to use the side streets. As Wednesday began I was sitting in my car, parked at the riverside and waiting patiently, like a poacher waiting for a rabbit. I wanted Alexander to come out of his house the back way and either turn to take the long walk down the main road into town or pass by me by taking the bridge, or even just hail a cab.

The change to the traffic system had finally alerted the parking wardens that there were vehicles parked in the area behind Adelaide Road. That morning I watched a warden arrive on a bicycle to start checking the cars for resident parking permits. I started up my car and reversed down the street, took a ten-minute detour further up the road and then returned to park again after the warden had gone.

Whoever heard of a copper paying to park anywhere? Except I wasn't playing that part any more, now that Mick had finally twigged. Perhaps it was my soft hands and soft face that had given me away, or perhaps it was intuition. Anyway, hats off to Mick, whom I felt represented pretty standard opinion. I wasn't a copper any more, just a gumshoe doing his job.

I didn't see Alexander again for nearly ten days. As I couldn't make any progress, eventually I gave up on the case entirely. I was disgusted that my career had hit such a low. I'd sat in my car for days, getting backache, watching mums pushing prams, or joggers, or old people walking their dogs: any excuse, I felt, to be nosey and keep tabs on me. I'd been hired to watch Alexander, by whom I no longer knew, but I can't do the impossible if the mark chooses to disappear.

I'd read Alexander's journal so many times I was sick of it and thought about returning it to him. I understood much more of his character now and understood that he liked to see meaning in every moment. In one extract he was musing about that bloody blind that had tumbled from his window.

Fortunately, the window blind missed my new ink pen, an expensive engagement present from Penny. I sat there for a moment after it fell, bemused at first, and then laughed like an idiot. Thank you, Emerson: I will pay attention. The weak October sunshine ducked below the clouds in a last play for dominance and the final few minutes of daylight lit up my face.

Penny: I wondered what had happened to her. She seemed to have been expunged from his life. I had thought that was that when he had moved on to Ruth and then Melanie. I didn't really blame him. Some young men go through women like sex is going out of fashion.

There was now a steady stream of people passing me as I sat in my car, all heading over the bridge towards the city centre. It was now November 5th, a Saturday. Bonfire night had arrived and with it a universal desire to watch fireworks. I stopped cursing Alexander's absence and decided to join in. I put the journal in the glove box, locked the car, and texted my wife. She was at her sister's, so we agreed I needn't go home until later.

The first thing I did when freed from the confined space of my Citroen was to walk up the side street by the Hay Wain and stop to look at the site of the garage.

A big bulldozer rumbled past me and drove down the main road in a cloud of blue smoke. The machine turned the corner and stopped at the rear of the site. A worker jumped off, clad in yellow hat and jacket, and moved some cones so that the snorting bulldozer could enter the site.

A backhoe loader was next, this one a more nimble machine, moving more like one of those fast dinosaurs my son liked when he was young. It parked in the side road at the front of the former garage forecourt, opposite Alexander's house. Then a white van arrived and parked at the rear of the garage and out jumped half a dozen hard-hatted builders, all young men who spoke a foreign language.

The bulldozer lowered its blades and picked up a few remaining bits of brick and masonry in its bucket. A lorry appeared and the bulldozer deposited its load in the back of it, raising a cloud of dust. The backhoe loader started to dig a trench parallel with the street. I stood watching, amazed at how quickly a landmark can be erased; how easily it can be replaced with something new.

All that was left of the showroom was a low wall. The enormous reflective glass windows had been removed, so now any casual observer could see inside. The wooden stool was still there in the exact position I had left it. I remembered Alexander talking about an orchestra when he'd been speaking to his therapist, standing mere feet from where I had been listening from behind the glass. Alexander's journal entry on the subject talked about people and their real identity. It was an entry I'd read many times, I was so taken with it.

'Only a few pedestrians were out on the street. I didn't know what animal they were. They looked a bit like me. Some stood outside the garage opposite, waiting, ready to cross the street. They looked worried or not worried, depending on their type. Then they moved quickly out of the way of the river traffic, to disappear out of view beneath me: perhaps into Mick's store or the sub- Post Office on my side of the road. But it was only ever at the garage opposite that anyone ever stopped to present their real identity, stood still by a pump, patiently filling up their car. Then they paid the Chinese lady or fat man at the counter behind the blue door and left the garage, always feeling just a little bit more assured and relaxed after their stop. I imagined some of the customers did spare a moment to wonder why and to question what went on in the other half of the garage, the right-hand side with large reflective windows and a white door with the sign Forecourt Watch – Keep Locked. But nothing was visible through the curved glass windows save their own distorted reflections, as if they felt embarrassed looking at themselves. Thus the inquisitive were kept at bay by their own vanity, to be sucked back into the River Traffic, to swim furiously for their lives.'

The writing was dense, imaginative, questioning and self-aware. But what was Alexander's point, what was he saying? He seemed to want people to slow down, to stop, and take a moment to contemplate their own existence. Was he a religious man? I wasn't sure after the night with Ruth in the wine bar and the argument with Christos outside the church. Perhaps the sight of people driving about, stopping to refuel and then driving about again annoyed him. Perhaps he saw their whizzing about as a mindless, mundane activity. He had higher aims: the study of beauty, not least the study of beautiful women. He also had the amazing capability of generating art from the responses of a subject exposed to beautiful experiences. I remembered my own experience in the white room vividly and would have dearly liked to repeat it, perhaps this time in his presence. I would also have liked to have seen Penny again to talk to her, not just to leer at and lust after her, as I was now ashamed to have done in the market square. I'd like the chance to talk to her about Alexander and what made him tick, which after all was what I was getting paid for.

A more and more complex picture of Alexander was forming in my mind. He was a man who could see the truth; he was a guru, a professor. It was Alexander who had to put people straight on the facts: for example, Christos and his followers in the bookshop, who believed they could communicate with the Holy Spirit. But Alexander seemed to possess a power that showed him they were wrong; he could see the emptiness of what they were saying: that actually it didn't make any sense. Alexander thought that the windows of the garage showroom were a reflective veil that hid another world, beyond which lived those who could touch the real truth. Perhaps, I thought, he'd seen the Wizard of Oz.

Alexander wanted to be like his hero, Nabokov; he wanted either to have, or somehow to acquire, a quality called synaesthesia. With a synaesthetic viewpoint of the world Alexander could receive visions of the truth. If you didn't understand what this was about you couldn't join Alexander's club and he wouldn't be your friend. Melanie was OK because in Alexander's perception she was beautiful and had a halo.

I'd written all this down for my client to read, as was my brief.

Unexpectedly, there was the man himself. Alexander had appeared, walking down the road towards the bridge that crossed the river with Melanie on his arm, holding his journal in his other hand.

I watched from the car as Alexander and Melanie joined the crowds walking into the city centre to watch the fireworks. Alexander could do normal things as well, I wrote down. I conjectured that in the weeks that he'd been away, out of my sight, he had been forming a healthy bond, potentially even a lasting relationship, with Melanie.

The happy couple, and they did look happy, passed at a good distance from where I stood, partially hidden as I was behind a lamppost in the side street. I could see their faces, Melanie still wearing her trademark blue beret. I gave them a one-minute head start, enough time for them to cross the river and reach the other side, and then I climbed out of the car and followed them.

They were headed for a pub by the river. It was crammed with people when they arrived; I followed them into the pub's garden, dropping a couple of coins into the white charity bucket. We all three entered just as the fireworks display began. The first rockets exploded and showered the sky with spheres of light followed by the sprinkles of a sparkling shower. I had on my woollen hat and a red scarf wrapped around my throat and mouth, the perfect disguise. It had been years since I had been out to see fireworks and I felt like a kid again. I quickly relearned the skill of anticipating the new, loudest fireworks, the ones that left the ground with a discreet pop, disappeared high up into the sky, and then, just as they seemed to have been lost, detonated with a colossal thump, startling the people gathered below.

There were maybe three hundred people watching the display, all jammed into a small area at the side of the river. Some were standing on the river bank by the road; others were closer to me in the pub garden, some even standing on the tables, though the pub staff made it clear they disapproved. Two men on the other side of the river, dimly visible through the drifting smoke, were in control of the spectacular that was exploding above us.

I realised Melanie and Alexander were now standing next to me. She looked a million dollars in a fur coat with a white stole around her neck and the inevitable blue beret.

'Thank you, Mr Cleary,' she said.

'Thank you, Melanie; it's nice to see you here.' He giggled and she kissed him on the cheek.

I turned my head away and hunched my shoulders so my face dropped another inch lower into my scarf.

'This is a great firework show,' said Melanie. 'Everyone loves it.'

'Makes you think, doesn't it, how easy it is to get people together.'

In order to carry on their conversation they had to shout over the din of the fireworks and the cries of the crowd.

'What is it that they most like?' asked Alexander. 'Which of these elements overhead is the manifestation of the Form of Beauty?'

'Or is it beautiful because people are together?' responded Melanie. 'Would we all enjoy this so much if we were alone?' She nibbled his ear. She was six inches shorter than Alexander (I'd say about five foot). If in the future my son were to find such an attractive girlfriend I'd be very pleased.

Melanie and Alexander were easy in their intimacy, respectful yet playful, shouting and laughing as the sky filled with colour and noise. The firework organisers were pulling out all the stops. The sky was alive with fireworks; dense smoke was drifting down the river.

Melanie took off her gloves; the nails of her ringed fingers shone with a soft bluish light. Alexander took her hand. 'What is this sorcery?'

'Fluorescent nail-polish,' she said and waved her hands, tracing a bluish trail in the air like a plane writing a message in the sky.

Their conversation was curtailed by the finale of the fireworks show. The sky became filled with coloured explosions for many protracted minutes. The piece de resistance came when a giant Catherine wheel was ignited. It spun round, gaining speed, until each of its fuses had been lit and it was burning. The crowd cheered and clapped. Some people standing on a bridge downstream let off a few rockets of their own. They were illuminated by the huge spinning wheel. We applauded until the Catherine wheel slowly fizzled out. It finally came to a stop. There were to be no more surprises.

'That was great!' said Alexander.

'Brilliant!' agreed Melanie. Then she looked at her hand, concerned.

'What is it?'

'One of my rings.' She inspected a gap on one of her heavily bejewelled fingers. 'I must have lost it when I took my gloves off. I hope I can find it.'

The happy couple crouched down and looked around on

the ground. Before they could ask me to help I moved away. I didn't want to risk being recognised from the prayer meeting in the church.

'Oh, never mind about it.' Melanie smiled at Alexander. 'Look, the pub has a couple of punts. Let's go punting! Come on, one of them is free.'

It was the second occasion on which I had seen I a look of uncertainty cross Alexander's face. The first time had been at the garage when he had fallen against the showroom window, seemingly afflicted by some weakness. That incident had passed quickly enough; and so, too, this second time, after a brief wobble, his face had regained its colour and his eyes their sparkle as he gamely agreed to Melanie's plan. They beat everyone else to the last available punt. Alexander paid the chauffeur and helped Melanie into the rocking craft.

I bought a pint of beer from the bar as I watched them cast off and follow the line of other punts downstream. I hoped they'd have a good time. I was expecting them to disappear out of sight in an elegant fashion, leaving me to enjoy my pint, eat a hot dog, and get home before the pubs chucked out so that I could evade the police out on the highways looking for drink-drivers.

But Alexander was in difficulties. He quickly became nervous and distracted by the task of propelling the punt, which seemed in his hands to have gained a weight dispropor- tionate to its size. Somehow he'd turned the punt 90 degrees so that it was now across the width of the river, one end hidden in the weeds against the bank. I wasn't the only one who found it amusing. Giggles floated on the air as people noticed his predicament. Sad to tell, Alexander, the great man, the great artist, punted like a hopeless beginner. His solution to rescuing the punt from its position against the bank was to sink the long pole deep into the river, using it as an anchor, and then press down with his body weight. He hoped that this would succeed in returning it to its proper course.

Melanie looked smaller when she was sitting in the punt. She was at the front, probably nervously calculating the likelihood of having to take a swim.

They had drifted out from the bank but the pole remained stuck in the river bed. Alexander was having trouble in letting it go. Soon he would be left clinging to the pole like a koala bear in a tree. With all his might and no doubt considerable consternation, Alexander pulled the pole from its watery socket, lifted it clear out of the river and trailed it across the punt. Water cascaded down its length and splashed on to Melanie. There were some in the crowd who laughed. I just watched, shaking my head, embarrassed for Melanie.

Alexander seemed to be both annoyed and getting very angry at how events were turning out. This unfortunate and embarrassing situation would have tested anyone. Get a grip, man, I thought, take control. Alexander redoubled his efforts, leant on the pole and, with a great surge of energy, pushed the punt out into mid-stream. Unfortunately, the result was that they shot straight across the width of the river to the other bank. Frantically he turned the punt parallel to the bank, again pushing down and straining on the pole, then jumped out and made it fast by tying the rope around a willow tree. He seemed unaware of the fact that Melanie was now caught under the wet branches of the willow, the fronds of its branches scratching her face.

But there had been no major mishap. Alexander held the punt still and pulling back some of the offending branches, helped Melanie crawl out of the punt to dry land on the bank, where she lay down doubled up with laughter. Amazingly, Alexander still mustered enough strength and presence of mind to lie on his back and write in his journal.

I watched as they lay on the ground together, looking up at the smoke drifting across the sky. They had amused the crowd, which had offered a smattering of applause. In some ways they'd passed a test, a sort of coming-out in public, and the crowd approved: even though Alexander clearly couldn't punt to save his life, he did have a pretty girlfriend. All the world loves a lover. Now they were both on their hands and knees and laughing so hard they couldn't get up. He kissed her on the cheek, then the lips, and again they lay down together in the long grass.

Even from my vantage point some way beyond the river bank I felt embarrassed by their intimacy, but I dutifully recorded the scene in my diary. The subject and a lady friend, identified earlier as Melanie, enjoyed an evening of fireworks at one of the public houses along the river. After the event, Mr Clearly treated Melanie to a punt trip across the river. They made a fine-looking couple and were popular with the crowd, which they'd entertained with some unorthodox manoeuvres on the river. If I might break from protocol, Alexander came over as a knight and Melanie as his princess.

What client wouldn't be pleased with such a description?

CHAPTER 14

I WALKED AWAY from the pub and took up a place downstream on the bridge. From there I could see the happy couple standing on the far bank next to their punt, first pointing up and then pointing down river. There was something agreeable about being a distant observant eye watching over my client as he went about his business.

Sports psychologists say that if you want to win an event visualise yourself as a separate person whom you can see actually winning the event. Don't limit yourself with the fears and anxieties of the 'me'; instead, view yourself as the bold and fearless 'I'. In other words, be the person other people see and win that event!

Alexander gave Melanie his hand as she stepped back into the punt. There was a sudden rocking and a rattling of the chain at the front of the punt as she got in which almost capsized it. They nearly lost the wooden pole, which at one point began to float away on the current. Melanie reached out and grabbed it and gave it to Alexander so he could keep them moving. She wiped her wet hands on her jeans and sat back to relax. Alexander stood up, scribbled briefly in his journal, and tried his skill again.

He was steadier the second time round. Alexander took the punt on an easier course mid-river, using up a lot of water but heading in the right direction and avoiding the banks. They were approaching the bridge I was standing on. I bent down to tie my shoelace and stayed hunched down like a troll. I had become someone who merely watches and waits, a cypher.

The punt passed underneath the bridge. 'You could come back to mine, if you like,' I heard Melanie say. Her words rang as clear as day as I contemplated the wood and ironwork of the bridge. Peeping out through the slats of its walls, I saw the top of Melanie's blue beret and then the thick black hair on the top of Alexander's head as they passed underneath. I caught a glimpse of the look on his face: he was concentrating hard, his eyes darting everywhere, taking into account all the potential hazards on his chosen downstream course. But he was growing in confidence, standing strong-legged on the stern, propelling from the side of the craft. He now had enough courage to take the pole out of the water, shimmy it up his hands and strike it down on the other side of the boat. At one point, floating downstream, following the middle of the river perfectly, he took the pole fully out of the water and held it under one arm and outwards in front of him, like a knight's lance. He said in a loud, clear voice:

'In this moment of revelation, he sees his connection to all things, and also contains all variety within his own being. I become a transparent eyeball; I am nothing; I see all; the currents of the Universal Being circulate through me; I am part or parcel of God.'

I saw a rapturous look appear on Melanie's face. Her perfect mouth opened and her blue-rimmed eyes shone bright. 'That was beautiful,' she said.

'Ralph Waldo Emerson,' Alexander said. 'He was a transcendentalist. He believed in the pantheistic notion of the spiritual unity in all things, the belief that the absolute entity can be grasped by intuition alone.'

'Do you believe that?' she asked.

'Something like it,' he replied.

They drifted on, now floating away from me. It was ten o'clock. The night air was chill, the moon had risen fully, and their craft had left a silvery wake in the water. I had frozen into a hunchback on the bridge, mesmerised by Alexander's straight back and Melanie's blue beret. Perhaps it was the reflective surface of the water that allowed the sounds of their voices to reach me so clearly.

'Where is your place, then?' I heard him say.

I could see her take off her beret and smooth back her blonde hair with both hands. She sounded happy, in her voice a mixture of relief, excitement and certainty. 'It's about three miles away in the middle of nowhere, but it's nice, the river runs really close.'

'I didn't know you were a local girl?'

'There's a lot you don't know about me.' And that was the last I could make out as the sounds of their voices were lost in the lapping of the river near me as it slapped at the sides of the banks.

Creakingly, I straightened myself up. Now standing, I was still watching them from the bridge. If they saw me, they would attach no significance to a man on the bridge, his collar up and a scarf wrapped around his head, even if Melanie spotted me, remarked on it to Alexander and he turned around. Through my opera glasses, which I had pressed back into service because the German field glasses had not arrived, I saw Melanie take a packet of cigarettes out of her jacket pocket. She offered one to Alexander, who shook his head. She lit a cigarette with a lighter produced from within her fur coat and placed the filter in her mouth. The small flicker from the lighter illuminated her smiling face. She was in love.

I could, and perhaps should, have left them to it. But I'd just seen a chauffeured punt drop off a party of four on my side of the river. The young punter, wearing a straw boater and a gold waistcoat, was waiting on the bank hoping for further customers. I hailed him immediately, gladly paying him the twelve pounds for a round trip. I could let my hair down a bit as there were now only two days left on this assignment. Alexander and Melanie had made me feel young again.

I told my chauffeur to follow the punt in front and he nodded as if he heard such a request all the time. I sat back and enjoyed the thrill of the experience. I'd spent too many days sitting about either in that garage or in my car while I was watching Alexander. It was really good to get out and experience some of his world. That was why I was hired, and I believed in doing a good job. I am a finisher, everyone always agrees on that, tenacious, like a bulldog.

My chauffeur asked if I wanted to hear some stories about the history of the river and I accepted his offer. So it was I heard a good yarn about Rupert Brooke, who apparently used to commute into the town, as it was then, by canoe, travelling up the river from one of the famous villages, the slip-slip of his paddle cutting through the leafy secrets of the waterway. Houses with names like Paradise and Shangri-La were hidden in the bends of the river.

At a turning one of these famous villages was revealed. I paid my chauffeur another ten pounds to take me further along the route, still following the happy couple. The young man readily took my money, at the same time texting someone with his mobile. Then he gave a huge pushing-off, using both hands. Once we were under way, he produced a cigarette that carried with it a faint whiff of cannabis. My man was an expert and showed off some one-handed propulsion as he enjoyed his spliff. I sat back, relishing the ride, looking back to watch our slipstream. When I looked over my shoulder I could see Alexander and Melanie gliding along splendidly up ahead. At one point, I asked the chauffeur to swap places and to punt from the front of the boat, and my man, with the merest shrug, agreed. Both standing up, we managed to manoeuvre past one another so that now I was sitting at the stern and better able to keep an eye on my targets up ahead.

We sailed merrily along following perfectly the curve of the river, the smoke of my chauffeur's cigarette curling up from under his straw boater. I was aware that we would be bound to overtake Alexander and Melanie in the next few minutes. I had to come up with a plausible reason for being out on the river this late at night and in such a remote location.

'Any more stories?' I asked him, but this time in a slight American accent. 'I so love this place,' I added, using the same accent for the benefit of Alexander and Melanie, who were now within earshot.

My chauffeur told me about the Bloomsbury Group and how they liked to take a trip, which they called a jolly, out to the sticks. Virginia Woolf and Maynard Keynes would be downing champagne and oysters, washing away their wordy contests with Darjeeling tea at the Orchard Tea Rooms, or chatting over beer at the Green Man; or perhaps they would decide to halt at some point on the river bank for a picnic.

We slid silently past Alexander's punt. I had once again turned up my jacket collar to hide my face and I was still wearing the hat and scarf.

'Evening all,' called out my chauffeur.

'Hello,' said Melanie.

And my chauffeur powered on by. We glided along, slowing as we turned a corner in the river, now drawing away from Alexander, who nevertheless was doing a good, workmanlike job.

I heard a phone ringing in their punt, the musical ringtone twittering across the water. Alexander stopped punting, turning his craft back towards the bank. I feared another disaster. One hand was in his pocket as he pulled out his phone. Then there he was, looking sad, as he contemplated the number on the display.

'Hello,' he said.

I could hear a woman's voice coming from the phone. 'Hello. How are you?' said the voice.

'Yes, I'm all right. You OK?'

'Yes.'

Alexander and the caller maintained silence for a few seconds. I could still see his face as our punts drew apart. The sound of voices carries incredibly well across water. It's like speaking against a mirror and seeing your breath reflected on the surface.

'Are you there?' I recognised the voice; those well-rounded tones, that slightly cross timbre were unmistakeable. For some reason Alexander had put his phone on speaker and was broadcasting the conversation across the river.

'Yes,' said Alexander.

'Good,' replied Penny. I was certain it was she.

My chauffeur had now turned the corner of the river and was pushing the pole down into the river bed with firm, even strokes, powerfully driving us along. I wanted to tell him to stop so that I could hear more, but I couldn't make it so obvious that I was eavesdropping.

'How's life?' I heard Alexander ask. That was the last sentence I could make out. To my chauffeur's consternation, I stood up again, although I was now at the front of the punt, and saw that Alexander's punt was once again sliding into the river bank. There was a clunk as Alexander dropped his phone on the floor of the punt, grabbed the pole with both hands and thrust it into the side of the bank like a knight slaying a dragon, but it was too late to save this princess. Melanie squealed and put her arms over her head as the craft crashed through the weeds and came to rest among the overhanging branches of a willow tree.

We heard their laughter, my chauffeur and I, as we looked back and saw them both tangled up in the skirt of the willow. We saw Melanie pick up the phone and hold it under her chin. 'Boo!' she said, framed in the green light. She turned the light on Alexander, who laughed as he turned the phone off.

'Kids!' I said, 'made of rubber.' My chauffeur agreed that they would be fine. We travelled on, my chauffeur's spliff relighted. The scenery along the banks of the river was changing, the hedges giving way to a more open view of the surrounding fields. We continued to push on down the river, sidling past the concrete pill boxes built to defend the country against Operation Sea Lion, past hay barns and tractors standing silently in the fields.

When we came to the first house – it was on the left bank – I asked my man to pull over. He was clearly relieved to be able to take a break. I thanked him for his help and said that he could leave me there. Underneath his rolled-up sleeves I could see red patches on his arms: I wouldn't have been surprised if he'd been punting all day. I tipped him an extra twenty, which pleased him a great deal, and gently he made off even further up the river, heading for some unknown landing point. By the time Alexander and Melanie reached the spot where I'd got out of the punt I was already on the road, walking away.

I realised now that if I really wanted to portray Alexander in his true lights my role would be more akin to that of a stalker than a traditional private detective. It didn't take a genius to surmise that Alexander was likely to spend the greater part of the next day in bed. With an uncomfortable shiver it occurred to me that some would say the task of objective observer and dissector of a man's personality was a role that should be reserved for God. The task I'd been set could prove attractive to many. Pay someone enough money and he or she would write your story; but would you be satisfied with it?

Quite a revelation had taken place for me on that quiet country road as I walked quickly away from the river, my way lit by the moonlight, occasionally turning back to make sure Alexander and Melanie weren't behind me. Whether my report had been commissioned by Alexander himself or his grandfather, presumably it would fall into his hands at some stage. What a feast my writings would present to that young narcissist!

I needed to make clear exactly what I thought about Alexander's character. I would write an uncompromising account of the impression he made on an outsider and hope that would be an end to whatever the problem was that he was torturing himself with: if, indeed, it was a problem, not a giant game.

I shielded my watch to prevent its glow from betraying

my whereabouts. It was eleven o'clock. I climbed up a slope, away from the road, and hid behind a tree. What a fright I would give them if I was discovered. Melanie's screams would carry across the countryside and the farm dogs from miles around would come running to protect her. However, the happy couple walked past me, still totally wrapped up in one another. After five minutes I returned to the road and followed them.

The road was rough, the surface untarmacked. It ran parallel to the river for a while and was then diverted to traverse the empty fields, now lit by the moon in a starry sky. The road narrowed and was enclosed by high banks and tall trees, their branches knitting together over our heads. The occasional lay-by had been introduced at the side of the road to allow a car to stop and let another through. It was in such a passing place that I stopped to listen. I wanted to be sure that their voices were still carrying away from me.

I hung back, making little (if any) noise in my rubber-soled shoes, wondering how the night would end. Melanie and Alexander were still talking loudly, giggling and laughing, not bothering to keep an ear out for anyone following. The tree-lined lane ended abruptly. Once again we were out in the wilderness, the road now bordered by fields with no protective hedges. The occasional menacing hulk of a farm machine came looming out of the dark. Silent now, we all crept past isolated houses and farms. There was no sign of life at any of them.

After forty minutes of walking I saw them stop ahead of me. They had halted at the gate of a farm. Melanie was stroking the head of a dog.

'Hello, Jake,' she said, scratching the collie's head, her nail varnish still faintly luminous in the dark.

'He likes you,' Alexander said, his pen once again moving across the pages of his journal.

She gave the dog a kiss on the nose. 'This is the Clarksons' farm, and this is Jake, their nicest dog. They keep the others inside at night.' She patted the dog goodbye and they continued on their way, still lit by the moonlight and the lights of the occasional houses we passed. They bounced along in good spirits, frequently bumping into one another and then moving apart again, like billiard balls that were attracted but could not stay together. Finally, Alexander put his arm around her and pulled her close. They stopped to kiss and I turned round, hiding my white face from the moonlight. I stayed like that, still and silent, until I heard them laugh again and move on.

At midnight a pub called the Fox came into view. It was bathed in yellow light, some noisy party going on inside. Alexander and Melanie walked straight past it. My feet were killing me, which I thought was funny because as a plod you'd think I would be good at plodding. I'd no properly formulated idea of what I would do when they reached their destination, which I presumed to be Melanie's house.

The beauty of the surroundings was enchanting. I followed the happy couple quietly past several old houses. I was alive to their history and that of the honestly-worked land around them. A fox stopped in front of us in the middle of the road, its glassy eyes lit up by the moon, and disappeared as quickly as it had come.

There was a sharp bend, after which a track came into view, a white gate barring it from the road. There was a sign: Granary Farm. Melanie took Alexander's hand and led him down the farm track. You could see she was in charge; he wasn't unwilling to follow, but it was clearly her plan and her place. I hung back, thinking that this might well be it for the night. What would Alexander say if I revealed that I'd followed him further than the threshold of the farm? He would surely have regarded it as a breakdown of client-provider trust. I was already on dangerous ground, my own motives questionable: even though I wanted to do a good job and to please my client I wanted the money more.

I stayed where I was, one hand on the metal bar at the top of the gate; it was cool to the touch in the moonlight. I wished the happy couple well. I wrote the final paragraph in my notebook, the ink clear under the moonlight, finishing with a line about how they had ended their evening sailing down the river into the sunset.

I had revised my estimation of Alexander again. He might well be attracted by and interested in beautiful women but he was no Lothario. He might well have run his way quickly through Penny and Ruth but that was the clue, wasn't it? My client was becoming initiated in the ways of love and sex; I had no wish to write about that. If I could reach home and write my report the next morning, I would simply state that the client and his girlfriend headed towards a certain village where it was believed the young woman resided. I would exaggerate the gentlemanly conduct of the client, the loveliness of his girlfriend, and stress my professionalism by making it clear that I hadn't looked any further into their relationship.

I saw them appear under the farmhouse lights, which cast big shadows against the flint and stone walls. A key scraped in a lock but then they seemed to change their minds about what they were going to do and hurried away from the main building to a large hulking structure further down on the left of the track. There were more giggles and hushing sounds.

Melanie was dragging Alexander up to the top of a hay barn.

I could only hear fragments of noise: not speech, more like animal sounds, but made by humans. I imagined the barn was warm and peaceful, full of hay and straw stockpiled against the winter. They must have climbed a ladder: I could see their figures just under the eaves of the roof, presumably on some form of an internal floor high above the ground.

Something resembling an animal skin was flung from the barn. It opened up briefly as it dropped to the ground, unfolding its flightless arms. I saw that it was Melanie's fur coat.

I had turned my back on the barn and was walking away from the gate when the inevitable sounds reached me: two piercing squeals in quick succession. Sounds that could have been made by night animals. Someone in the farmhouse turned on an upstairs light, maybe thinking the same thing. I had no intention of being apprehended, a peeping Tom, outside their property. I had seen nothing, but of course could imagine it all. Melanie dressing silently, an indulgent look on her face, Alexander pulling his trousers up. I couldn't bear to think about the look on his face.

They would be holding hands. Alexander would help Melanie down the straw-baled stairway and they'd leave the barn without a word. There was the scrape of a heel on stone, then the squeak of the farmhouse door opening, a single hushing sound from a third party and then a dull click.

I walked on, heart pounding, glad to get away from the farmhouse lights. The semi-darkness returned, relieved only by the light of the moon. The road glowed grey and silver; I followed it on without a clue where I was going. The night air was fresh and my breath emerged in small clouds as I exhaled. I permitted myself a small laugh. The sound echoed from the edges of the field. I could also hear the little scratchings, scrapes and snaps of small unseen animals, but I felt at ease, happy that the assignment was over. I had gathered more than enough evidence to satisfy my client's vanity. Alexander was as normal a young man as you would hope to meet. He was on an adventure, finding out who he was and who he wanted to be. I would toast him with the first of many cocktails when I reached Florida.

I became alerted to the noise of people talking up ahead. A large house loomed into view, the lights from the windows dazzling my eyes. I stepped along smartly, the cold creeping in under my coat and hat, ready with a story if anyone asked me. I'd say it was my habit to take a stroll in the early hours.

None of this new group of people was interested in me because they were all half-cut. They were just emerging from yet another pub. I couldn't believe my luck: I saw that a party of three had called a cab to head back into town. I introduced myself and offered to pay the fare if they'd let me accompany them, playing the American tourist again. I succeeded in taking them in completely.

We drove up the main road, where there was a surprising amount of traffic. I gave my name as Mickey and told the other three passengers that I owned a luxury car showroom on the north edge of town. One of the men knew more about cars than I could wish so I had to do my best to remember what I could about a friend's father's Jaguar. The lone woman sitting in the back observed that I looked young to own a showroom. I had to agree that I was young as well as lucky. I admitted to having had a privileged upbringing in Florida. They were very taken with the idea.

The driver dropped the three revellers off at the castle and then carried on up the ring road towards Alexander's house, where I had parked my car. I was tempted to take the cab all the way to where I lived outside town but the meter was already displaying a worryingly high fare. There was nothing for it but to pick up my car and drive home: I was OK with that: my one pint of the evening was long since metabolised. When the taxi stopped at the back of Alexander's house I saw that my car was still there, waiting faithfully for me. I tipped the driver a couple of quid and he drove off, very pleased. Disguises, accents, all part of the job; none of it from training, all from experience, together with a curiosity about how people act and respond to strangers who act with authority. You can tell people all sorts of things; most people are quite naïve.

I drove home, where my wife was sitting up in bed reading a holiday brochure. I told her that I'd completed the last evening of surveillance, that in the morning I would stay at home and write my final report. She gave me a hug; tired from a late evening at her sister's, she fell asleep quickly. I lay awake in bed for some time, the events of the evening's surveillance replaying in a loop. Even if I'd wanted to, I wouldn't have been able to forget it.

CHAPTER 15

B Y THE TIME I got up late on Sunday morning my wife had left the house to visit a friend who was poorly. I would be able to retrieve the torn-up photograph of Penny that was still hidden in the journal's pages. I also set out Nabokov's autobiography, a book I thought that I would force myself to read in the hope of gaining added insight for my final report about Alexander.

Sitting at the kitchen table, where I always preferred to work if I could and with a mug of tea in my hand I looked back at the case. I thought about how Alexander might similarly be sitting at his desk at this very moment, unaware of how a private eye hired to watch him was now preparing his final report. If, of course, Alexander wasn't still in the farmhouse enjoying sun-coloured egg yolks and free-range pork sausages prepared by Melanie's mother, the lucky bastard. I was aware that Alexander had provided me with an impressive finale. Now he would want his performance written up in such pleasing prose that in years to come, when he was an old man, his adventures long since ancient memories, he would read of his exploits as a young rake and feel that truly he had lived life to the full.

I raised my cup of tea to him: so be it, I would make him look amazing.

I worked on my report throughout the morning. I made a concerted effort to remember all the details of the previous day. Then I drew a line connecting all the facts on paper which provided me with a working narrative. By midday I had written out a draft in long hand, at which point I got up from the table, stretched, and noticed there had been a change in the weather. It had started out as a nothing day weather-wise, but now it was raining and a strong wind had started to blow outside. I became quite perturbed by this wind which was rattling the windows, seeming to encircle the house as if it might blow down the chimney. It was a very noisy wind, whooshing in a steady crescendo, then fading, then coming back at me again.

The weak sunlight that appeared also annoyed me; the clouds, driven across the sky by the wind, produced alternating dull and bright moments, straining my eyes with the sudden shock of renewed sunlight.

I'm an outdoors man really, despite the time I'd spent so pleasurably in that showroom; normally I don't like being trapped inside a building. I had enjoyed the walk the night before as well as – especially as – the cruise down the river.

I went upstairs and to the room at the left of the landing, which is usually locked, and found the key to it in the bathroom cabinet. I clicked the 'on' switch of the boiler in the airing cupboard to make the heating come on. It took twenty minutes to warm myself up, all the time pressing my hands on the top of one of the radiators.

When I returned to the table to re-read my draft I was disappointed. There were facts but there was no flow. I really was a plodder, an ex-copper turned private dick, a man who thought as well as typed one finger at a time. Reading and writing isn't really my thing but sheer determination is, so

I laboured away with the steady matter-of-fact description of my client and his ways until by three o'clock there were enough ingratiating highlights in the report to satisfy the most narcissistic of men.

I had an extra reason to feel pleased with myself: I knew there was a chicken and ham pie and some chips in the freezer. I popped them in the oven, mouth filling with saliva at the sight of the illustrations on the packets. Perhaps I had chosen the right path in life, one of simple action not one of words. When I was hungry, I ate food, pretty much any food, but you couldn't call me a foodie. When someone wanted something doing, I'd roll my sleeves up or put on my coat, hat and scarf and go and do it. The house was now toasty warm and the smell of the pie in the oven very appealing. The wind still rattled the windows and played a strange note across the top of the chimney but it didn't annoy me anymore.

The lunch was fine: it perfectly resembled what Nigel in the Hay Wain could conjure up with the same ingredients. I made myself another mug of green tea and formulated a plan. I had completed the second draft of my final report. I had in my possession Alexander's journal, the photo of Penny and Nabokov's autobiography. There was just half a day of this assignment to go and then I was done. I would have completed two solid weeks' work even if they were not on contiguous days. As agreed in the contract there had been fourteen full days of observation.

For one last insight and to check I hadn't missed anything, at random I opened a page of Alexander's journal. This entry caught my eye:

God: the word conjured blackness, its spoken image driven hard by the initial letter g was the black of space, but it was not a complete black, a philosophical or physical void, or a nothing. Instead it was a slightly pliable, almost rubbery black that suggested that there was something in the darkness. The ivory o and the walnut d were brief blips of light in the gloom: the bone and wood of Nature.

God again and this weird salad of the senses called synaesthesia, a condition which he seemed to have or at least wanted to have, like his hero Naboko.. It was very difficult to figure out what was real with Alexander. I would have given a lot simply to sit down at my kitchen table and talk to him. That would have made all the difference.

I flipped through his journal again, looking for entries about the God question. On many pages he had written long additional sentences set out in a rectangular line around the margins; sometimes they straddled pages. They were exceptionally long sentences and required me to turn the journal around in stages as if I were turning the wheels of a car. It took me a long time to get anywhere with these sentences and even longer to make them mean anything.

Here was one entry, which somehow I had missed in previous readings:

Dreadful to say it, but occasionally even I get tired of the great search to know God, to seek him out. Sometimes I think I should just stop.

Then on the next page, written around its margins:

But I can't stop. The philosophers will not find him, nor will the scientists; they will only explain him away. I could simply leave the defence of God in the hands of certain theologians, Barth, for example, who wanted to hide God away, free from the persistent and upsetting search of the radical. Karl Barth had it right when he wrote "Totaliter aliter. God is the wholly other, there are no points of contact between us and him." And so Barth hid God safely away from man.

Then there was a drawing of a darts-board-style target in the upper corner of the page: a simple target with an outer and an inner circle and a bull's eye. I remembered that I'd noticed this page before. An arrow had been drawn in flight, flying towards the target.

Bother Spinoza and his Ethics. His silly ontological argument that God existed necessarily, because at most only God can exist and all other things existed by being in God. The low flat bruise of the sky presses down heavily on the grey smokiness above the trees. All of this: the wind, the rain, this house, and people everywhere, were all in God.

I paused and looked outside. I imagined Alexander at his desk writing these words, the same weather outside.

Spinoza was clever. He came up with a clever defence for use by those who wished to hide God away from the radical man who might like to deconstruct or dismantle him. His idea was not to hide God outside the universe, like Barth's, but to hide God right in front of our noses, within the universe, because God was the totality of the universe. The point was to hide him in plain sight: and if God was found by the searcher (who was part of God) then God must exist, because the searcher existed: otherwise the searcher would be in the strange position of disbelieving his own existence.

I laughed a little at that bit. Even I, an uneducated man, could understand that. It reminded me of several crooks I'd nicked over the years who never knew anything about the stuff they'd stolen even when caught red-handed.

On the next page the arrow had been moved closer to the target. As I looked at it the wind outside rattled the windows and shook the last leaves off the trees. Outside it was strangely dark again.

The next three pages were decorated with the flight of the arrow along the top margin, moving steadily closer to the target. I kept turning the pages until I found the one where the arrow finally hit its target. Below it Alexander had written:

But of course there is contact between man and God! The artist understands the contact, and he is superior to the philosopher and the theologian. I am an artist and I will have my day.

I looked for further entries about this, eager to learn how Alexander would have his day. One thing I'd tumbled to was that for all his God talk, that's all it was: talk. There was only ever a lot of talk. There had been no religious icons anywhere in his house, nothing to suggest a sense of the other or belief in the beyond. I was also aware of how long ago it was since I'd managed to steal his journal. He must surely be missing it as well as Nabokov's book, the latter's return to the library now months overdue. I wondered if he gave even a second thought to Penny's photograph.

I couldn't second-guess my mark any further and I really did want his money and that holiday in Florida. Flattery of the man might be the answer. I decided that I would use his musings about God to demonstrate in my report that he was a thoughtful young man, a perception that he would surely appreciate.

Other evidence would concern his engagement with the Christians at the bookshop. He wasn't afraid to debate, to be ridiculed, to be the one against the many, the hero. I would point out that he had won the girl. He was a young man in need of praise and I could supply that for him.

My wife had returned so I stowed the journal away

amongst other books on the neat wooden shelves fixed against the white walls of my office. She came in through the front door, sodden and windswept, her long hair wrapped around her face. It made her look good. I helped her with her coat and umbrella and pushed the front door closed, shutting out the lashing rain. The hem of her skirt was so soaked that it had become a darker shade of pink than the rest of it; she went upstairs to change and I followed her. We laughed about the mad weather as she took a shower. I joined her and all was well in our little house.

CHAPTER 16

THE NEXT DAY was Monday. The week had started with a clear sky, the wind reduced to a ruffling breeze. I decided to go into town to find out a few details about place names and streets so that I could finish my report, completing the job as professionally as possible. I was particularly interested in retracing my steps through town to where Alexander had debated with the preacher Christos. I also wanted to figure out where in the village outside the town Melanie lived and the name of the house at which I had spied on them.

Before I left my house I looked at the calendar on the wall, noting the blue ring I had drawn around today's date. It marked the end of a difficult but well-paid project but it was also the anniversary of something else, one I had nearly forgotten. It was time to grow my business. I left the house thinking about how to get more work in the future.

When I reached my car I looked critically at the fading bodywork. The weeds seemed almost to envelop the wheels and decided that I needed a new motor. This car was OK but it wasn't reliable and I needed something that proclaimed me to be a successful man. I spent the morning at a local car dealer's, sitting in and then test driving the latest cars. All of the ones I chose were luxurious but extremely expensive. The dealer directed me to a rental business which he said might suit my needs better. I spent some time examining the cars there without arriving at any firm conclusions.

When I finally went into town I parked my car near the restaurant off the central park, the one where Alexander had met Ruth, and proudly displayed my disabled badge in the windscreen. It took me a while to find the church with the Christian bookshop outside it because on the evening when I'd followed Alexander and Melanie we'd all walked there from his house on the northern side of town. The bookshop was open, but I didn't go in. I looked up at the tower of the church and remembered that strange evening of the talking in tongues, of people letting go of their inhibitions and trying to communicate *en masse* with something that wasn't really there.

The market at the centre of the town was quieter than before. I stopped again at the cafe on the corner and ordered an espresso. I smiled at my memories of the day when Penny had appeared and blown everyone away with her looks. Now everyone and everything seemed grey and mundane; even the coffee wasn't quite hot enough. I opened my report and made a few neat amendments in pen. On the last page I wrote some nice things about Alexander, saying that he was a perfectly likeable young man with an enquiring mind and a magnetic personality. While it was my belief that his relationship with Penny had run its course I reminded my client that Alexander was young and in my opinion had handled the break-up considerately. I didn't mention the pornographic nature of the torn-up photograph fished from the recycling bin.

I had observed the process as he moved on to Melanie, whom he now seemed very keen on. Throughout the whole drama no-one had died, as they say in the movies, although I didn't write that in my report. I ended up wishing Alexander very well in his future life. Privately, I hoped that with the delivery of the report this would be the last I would hear of him. I wanted to move on to other, more straightforward cases.

I finished my drink and tipped the waiter generously. I must have been in a good mood or else I'd fancied myself still in the role of the American tourist. My report needed one more thing: a padded envelope to protect it; I bought one at a newsagent's. I weighed the package in my hand and thought about another package, that of an all-inclusive holiday in Florida.

From my pocket I took the letter from Mr Clearly Senior and inspected the route that had been drawn out so neatly for me. I was to start in the middle of the central park under a lamppost labelled 'Reality Checkpoint'. I was standing there now, in actual fact under four street lamps. The map I held took me towards one of the famous buildings that stood along the edge of the park, past the bright red post-box outside the police station, then across the corner of the park and down towards the bus station. I held the map in my hand, studying it, and following the directions again found an ancient brown wooden door in the wall to my left. The instructions described this as the 'north gate'. The door was heavy but when I shoved it with my shoulder I managed to make it budge. I entered what were evidently the grounds of one of the famous buildings.

The gardens beyond were green, beautiful and empty, the surface of the pond still and flat, several fine ducks sitting by its side. A bronze sculpture which appeared to be of a twisted, stylised mouth was shining in the morning sun.

The path my client had drawn for me wound through these impressive gardens, the magnificent drooping umbrella of a towering beech tree at its centre. It was here that I expected to meet my client; here I hoped to discover his real identity, and his true intentions; but there was no-one about and no-one appeared while I hung about underneath the beech tree feeling foolish. I walked on past the fragrant borders of red, pink and yellow roses which had been laid out under the protection of a high stone wall at the perimeter of the college. I came upon a small swimming pool set into the ground, its water deep and blue. Squashed into a small space at one end of the pool was a changing room, its walls heavy cotton sheets set in a timber frame.

I shook my head. Here I was in the middle of another world experiencing the bubble of another kind of life, the sort of existence that privileged people liked to boast about within five minutes of your having met them. I remembered that my wife and I had once watched a film about young men in white vests and shorts running around the inside quadrangle of a famous building. The point of the story was that one of their number finally achieved a world record in athletics. I could easily envisage those young men here now, clad in one-piece striped swimming costumes and sporting handlebar moustaches, running out of the hut and diving into the freezing water while the women, who would of course be dressed more demurely, sat at the edge and looked on. I almost expected Alexander and Penny to appear, or Alexander and Ruth – or now, perhaps, Alexander and Melanie. When I emerged from this reverie, all was still quiet; I was still alone.

The tranquillity of the place deepened as I walked further into the gardens. There were gentle noises coming from some of the old buildings: I could hear a flute in the distance, a bell tolling ten o'clock, the thwack of a squash ball on a squash court. At length I reached the main gates and effected my exit, managing to avoid the attentions of the suited man wearing a bowler hat who was sitting in the lodge. Above my head the flag above the gateway rattled, caught in a sudden gust of wind. It depicted a blue lion holding a ring of laurel leaves.

I carried on along the street, following the route on the map. The man I had presumed to be Mr Travis had met me at my house so he knew I wasn't exactly a local. Perhaps this hand-drawn map was just the result of an over-assiduous attempt to support me. However, I didn't really believe this, as my client had assumed I would be able to find Alexander's house with only the barest of clues. Why, then, was he being so helpful?

Of course the professed identity of my client had changed from Mr Travis to Mr Clearly Senior. From what I could remember of my first client, the one I had spoken to across my kitchen table, he bore no familial likeness to Alexander. How I rued not having taken a photo or other steps that would help to confirm his identity; I vowed not to make the same mistake again. He seemed too young to be anyone's grandfather. Perhaps Alexander resembled his mother or there was some other explanation. If Mr Clearly Senior was the true client he must have used the man I met as an intermediary. I had to assume he had a genuine interest in his grandson's wellbeing even if it was strange that he didn't know where he lived. He must have thought he had struck gold when he found me, a private detective living only a few miles away.

This had been quite an odd case, I had to admit. While I walked along I made careful notes in my notebook of everyone I encountered, especially those middle-aged men with hats or newspapers, the ones who might fancy themselves as characters in a detective novel.

The one-way road was busy; cars were queuing to leave the multi-storey car park, but I made my way down the pavement easily enough, mingling with the other pedestrians and the bicycles.

I passed a church with a bright nave window. Further church-like buildings popped out of the dusk. All of the buildings on this road were dark brown or grey. The wind picked up, hustling me down the street. There were dark metal weathervanes protruding from the towers and roofs. The air was warm and wet, perhaps signifying the prelude to a storm. I hurried past great façades of pollution-stained bricks and complicated runs of black drainpipes, past castle walls with narrow slit windows, guarded by heavy iron gates. I encountered signposts to university departments soberly inscribed in black and white paint, the whole city having adopted the same distinctive style. To my left, at the Museum of Archaeology and Anthropology, I glanced at the exhibition posters: they showed pictures of primitive masks howling with laughter, the faces painted to fight off demons. To my right, at the Holiday Inn, was a blander artwork, a smiling flower painted on a welcome sign.

I had reached a busy junction at which the road turned a sharp left to the river, creating a problem for those who wanted to head straight on to the very middle of the old buildings. I watched a young Chinese woman dressed in a red tracksuit and carrying a small rucksack on her back wheel her bicycle halfway across the road. Then she stopped, put up her hand and commanded the cars to do the same. The cars had indeed halted but were honking furiously at the girl. Unperturbed, she waved her comrades across the road, a dozen of similarly dressed and equipped students. When the last one had cycled over the junction she followed them, heading down Mill Lane towards the river.

All this walking and exercise provided a change from my usual solitary, sedentary occupations of observing and noting. It felt good to be out and about in the thick of it amongst the traffic and the crowds, happy in the knowledge that I had been involved in such an interesting case but glad that my stint was over. I would miss Alexander when the commissioned had been completed, but I looked forward to pay-day and toasting him with my wife as we lazed in the Floridan sunshine.

Something nagged at me, a little detail, a triviality that had caught my attention. I turned round to see a man wearing a trilby who ducked out of sight by hiding beyond the corner of a gentleman's outfitters. I noted the occurrence together with the idea that maybe, just maybe, I was being watched. I couldn't be sure of this, however.

I now found myself in a wide parade, a hundred onlookers able to watch me if they wished, including my real client. I could do little to safeguard against that possibility. I stopped outside the bank with the big red sign above it and paused a moment. This heralded the end of quite an amazing couple of weeks; it felt good to be alive.

Inside the bank I stood in line behind two people who were queueing at a teller's window clutching small red post-cards. We were all waiting for the only cashier who appeared to be on duty to become free. The customers ahead of me held out their driver's licences for identification, a practice which I found decidedly odd.

The cashier retreated to a large consulting room which we could see beyond the narrow area where the tellers' desks were arranged behind glass. This place was lined with many shelves.

Each time he returned with a different colleague to aid the waiting customer. Personal collection of items by customers who had stored them at the bank for safe-keeping seemed to be one of the main services used here. There was a small black camera in the ceiling. I looked at it only once.

Ten minutes passed while I read in Alexander's journal about the demise of his relationship with Penny Travis, being careful to keep the pages turned well away from the camera.

It is a relief for me today to move on. Penny will be pleased too: she will have no need to come into my studio again. Her face may now darken in her own room, in her own time, while I am left here sitting pretty on the velvet-legged stool, making progress with my art-generating device. I sigh as I think of all those struggles with her. She never did really understand what I was trying to achieve and, as time wore on, she made me doubt whether it would ever work. Nevertheless, each day I still experience the familiar leap of excitement in my chest when I wake and go into the studio. Perhaps today the machine will have something to show me: a small piece of artwork, perhaps, representing the first step on the road to communication. Nothing as yet, but disappointment does not mean a lack of progress, as neither does the lack of nonplussed looks from her. I will have to endure these no more. Look at today for the proof of what I am trying to do: four small triumphs outside my door, ready to do my bidding.

The cashier returned again. I was now first in the line and approached him at the counter, butterflies in my stomach, aware there were now five people waiting behind me and that they could hear everything I said.

I took out the journal from under my jacket, placed it in a

large brown envelope, sealed the top, and gave it to the cashier along with my client's letter. 'Here are the deliverables,' I said quietly, because I didn't want everyone to know my business. It was similar to the experience of ordering train tickets at a manned counter in a railway station. I'm not sure that the cashier heard me but he stuck a white label on the top right of the packet, handed me a paper receipt, and returned my client's letter to me.

I asked quietly about the fee I was due to collect.

'We haven't facilitated personal collection of funds for years,' said the cashier, a middle- aged Indian man, skin like stained mahogany.

'I see, yes I remember, it was to be by electronic bank transfer, my mistake.' I coughed and was unpleasantly disturbed by a constriction in my throat. I really didn't like discussing business matters in public.

On the other hand I was ready to be asked about it was like to be a registered private investigator, or even prepared to encourage him to want me to investigate a case on his behalf. Perhaps he would like me to check up on his wife and who she was seeing. However, I then saw that he lacked a wedding ring, although the skin on his ring finger had been worn down: it was lighter than the skin on the rest of his hand and shiny.

'Do you want to send this registered post?' the man asked. 'Is there anything of value in the package?'

Now that was a question! Fancy the cashier being so impertinent. But then I realised that the cashier was Yash, the owner-proprietor of the local post office on Adelaide Road. He appeared puzzled, turning the package over to inspect the delivery address and then back again to read the sender's address.

'Give it back to me,' I said quietly, and as requested Yash returned the envelope and letter to me. Keeping my appointment had been a failure. There had been a mistake in the payment instructions and I would have to sort matters out with my client.

'Next customer, please,' said Yash. I thought I could hear titters coming from behind me as I walked out into the sunshine.

I crossed the parade and sat on the wall outside another famous old building. There was much to think about.

I was glad of the comforting presence of my journal under my jacket. My report on Alexander for my mysterious client had finally been completed. All I needed to do now was to work out the best way of getting it to him. I had been working on this case for too long and I think I'd got a little hooked on it. People cycled past. People walked. I needed to slow down, to make myself think clearly.

I tried to figure out the latest developments. I didn't for one minute believe Mr Clearly Senior had written the last letter or that Mr Travis had ever been involved. I thought about Alexander's billowing white shirt, the six women in his life, the art-generating device in his house. This was a man who disregarded conventional boundaries. Once again I suspected that Alexander himself was my real client.

I walked back to my car, where a traffic warden stood looking at the details of the disabled sticker on the windscreen. I reassured him that I was the designated driver but that it was my brother who had the disability. Of course he didn't buy my story, but I slipped quickly into the driving seat and was soon driving away without his trying to stop me. However

I watched him from the rear mirror and saw him tap my registration number into his mobile. I knew within the next few days I'd get a parking ticket; I'd have to write it off as a necessary expense incurred doing the job.

I found the sign I was looking for when I reached the ring road and headed for the village where Melanie lived. I followed other vehicles along the long, narrow roads until gradually they all turned off and I found myself driving alone, turning my head occasionally to look out over the fields and the river. I noticed a bend in the river I thought I recognised and slowed down. Yes, this was the stretch of road we'd walked down that night; the road along which I'd stalked Alexander and Melanie; a fact of which I wasn't too proud, even though the project had demanded it. It was surprisingly long, I now realised. I slowed down, waiting for the gate and the track down to Granary Farm to appear. I stopped the car in a lay-by just before I reached the farm and completed the rest of the distance on foot. There was no-one about. At the end of the track stood the farmhouse which looked bigger in the daylight. Behind it and to the left was the hay barn. Good on 'em, I thought.

I remembered my first dates with my future wife. We liked to go driving in the country, top down on an old convertible I used to own back then, when I was still young and reckless and single. I used to race around the roads; the more twists and turns there were, the more thrilling the challenge. I imagined Alexander being like that with Melanie, driving her out to remote places, scaring her on the fast stretches of road but generally taking good care of her.

The vivid detail of these reminiscences surprised me somewhat. I was out here on my own, whiling away the time by filling in details like a novelist. I had stepped outside of my assignment and was beginning to lack focus. I needed to rein myself in and concentrate on the job in hand: I needed to get back on the case.

CHAPTER 17

I GOT BACK in the car and drove south on the main road out of town, heading home. As the sun set, I passed an old garage on the outskirts of the town. I had to look carefully to make sure Alexander wasn't there haunting the place, looking for strange things that weren't there. It struck me that for all his intelligence he was easily captivated by things that weren't true. I'm very much more of the what-you-see-is-what-you-get kind of person.

The car engine began to whine as the incline steepened. I was on one of the steep hills that guarded the southern entrance to the town; it was a good way of testing both my vehicle and my driving. I sat up in the driver's seat and willed the machine to carry on and up over that giant hill, knowing it was a serious challenge for my old, underpowered car. My car strained with every metre it climbed, with no respite in sight; it looked as if it had to keep on climbing forever. I felt my heart pounding and my head was hurting; I could feel a strange kind of headache coming on, caused perhaps by the noise of the straining engine or the vibration of the wheels on the road.

My car's attempt at the ridge of the giant's back was a valiant effort. I judged the gear changes as best I could and enjoyed the challenge of coaxing the car along. Changing from second gear into third we tackled the bottom of the hill, near to the base of the giant's spine. We built up the momentum; I kept my foot down, pumping the gas. The engine was screaming but to go into fourth gear now would have been a disaster. It was a mistake which I avoided. I paid no attention to the fact that there was now a long queue of cars behind, patiently following me up the giant's long body. I looked at the speedometer – thirty-five miles per hour – and smiled. I'd had this car a long time, serviced it myself, and it was repaying me for my care.

The neck and shoulders of the giant came into sight. Which one of the slumbering gods of old was it supposed to represent? Really, it was just a large bump in the ground, to the south of the town that called itself a city. The giant hunched its shoulders; the car screamed its way up to 40 mph. I kept it in third gear and on we charged.

There was a point on the hill near its crest when I wondered if we'd make it or whether the car would break down, expiring with a loud thump and a seizing of engine and gears. I was gripping the steering wheel so hard that the knuckles on my hands stood out as white ridges. It was a breathless moment; I felt at the mercy of the laws of physics. Would the car's momentum peter out and, after a moment of stasis, would it roll back down the hill? 35 mph: the speed was levelling out, other cars were passing me. My speed dropped to 30 mph as I reached the summit of the hill and triumphantly drove over the vanquished giant's head.

The car slowly picked up speed again as I eased the engine into fourth, conscious that the needle showing the engine's temperature had touched the red zone. Man and machine together relaxed like a racehorse who'd found its feet on the flat and was still bearing its rider. I sat back in my seat and, yes, I breathed a little easier, but I was unable to uncurl my hands from their obsessive clinging to the wheel and by now my head was pounding.

Someone sitting next to me coughed and said, 'It might be easier to drive if you didn't scribble in your book all the time.'

It took me a few moments to process the information and understand what was really happening. Melanie was sitting in the passenger seat, wearing a turquoise coat with a fur-trimmed collar and a blue beret and looking at me with wide eyes. I felt as if invisible messengers were running around my brain, each holding an urgent letter which, when I'd read them all, would enable me to piece together a rough draft of reality. Melanie, I must remember, was Alexander's girlfriend. Further messages were sent, read and acted on and from a distant part of my brain I retrieved another fact: I was Alexander. Action was then taken by the invisible scribes to rewrite my draft of reality, searching for a workable solution that could be presented to my uncomprehending mind. I was not the private investigator; I was Alexander. I had merely been pre-tending to be the PI. It was my final year project, something I'd engaged with to fulfil the requirements of my BA in Fine Art.

The scales fell from my eyes and my body went limp. Melanie laughed a little. 'Are you all right?' She sounded con-cerned and looked a bit scared as we continued the journey, her life in my hands.

I nodded and reassured her I was OK.

'It must be difficult to write and drive at the same time,' she said. 'I don't know how you do it.'

I changed gear and the pencil rolled off the journal / note-book and under my seat. I shrugged the journal / notebook off my legs so that it fell on the muddy and leaf-strewn foot mat.

'I didn't think we were going to make it up that hill,' she said, as a stream of cars accelerated past us.

Trees and fields flashed by as we headed to the best country pub I knew. 'The multi-tasking of voluntary action is extremely difficult,' I offered. 'Father used to check that Mother and I could rub our heads and also rub our tummies at the same time; I think he was worried about philosophical zombies.'

'Zombies?'

'It's the notion that people may look and act just like people but in reality they have no inner awareness or consciousness. They are just machines.'

'I'm pretty sure I'm not a zombie. I'd be happy to be a machine with awareness.' She looked out of the window and across the fields.

'Yeah, me too; trouble is you might just be saying the words like an automaton and as another automaton I would be too easily convinced you meant those words.' It occurred to me that I was undermining my own performance as her new and exciting boyfriend. But then Mother always said that if a girl really liked you, she would like you for yourself.

Melanie turned her head and pulled the fur lined collar up around her almond shaped face. The beret was an exact match to her burning cobalt eyes. 'You're a funny one.'

'A little bit funny, I agree.' I made an exaggerated gear change down into third as we turned a corner. 'This car has seen better days. It was Father's, he said it was cheap to run, but I'm not so sure.'

'Your Father? Is he still around?'

'Oh yes, and Mother, too. But no one else, I am an only child.'

We carry on down the hill, further out into the countryside.

'How far to the pub? I'm starving.' I noticed that she smelt good. At the very edge of my peripheral vision I could discern a fritillary butterfly.

'Five, ten minutes; it'll be worth it when we get there.'

'Alexander, why do you scribble in your book all the time?'

'I'm not scribbling. It's messy, but it's the real deal.'

'What is the real deal?'

'It's a journal for a project I'm working on.'

There was an open stretch on the road ahead, which was a dual carriageway. I stepped on the gas, trying to concentrate on the driving, but there was no chance of outmanoeuvring Melanie.

'Really? How interesting?' I didn't need to look at her to know there was no smile on Melanie's face now. The chequered brown wings tinged with silver and black had also disappeared. 'Am I in the project?'

'You make an appearance, yes.'

'Have you written about us having sex?'

'There is mention of it, but from a cerebral viewpoint. There's nothing the tabloids would get excited about.'

'Does your Father talk like that?'

I smiled and gave a little laugh. 'You are very smart.'

'For a farmer's daughter?'

'For my girlfriend, I haven't had many girlfriends as smart as you.'

'Ha, ha, that's not what the other girls had to say.'

'What girls?'

'All those nice women you had over to your house. Don't you remember? Or maybe you were too engrossed in your work.' Melanie shook her head. 'You pulled in a great catch of admirers on that day, and then ignored us all.'

I turned left at the sign for the Royal Oak and carried on down another long country road. We passed expensive houses, vast properties with outbuildings and stables. Melanie seemed particularly taken with one farm. It was surrounded by fields with cows. 'Nice big dairy farm, I'll have to ask Dad if he knows the family out here.'

I saw the pub sign up ahead, a spreading oak tree on a hill of old. It portrayed a typical English myth: Merrie England. We got out of the car with me listening to the radiator fan whirring. I touched the bonnet and found it was scalding hot.

'Patrick could fix that for you if you like.' She stood there, a moll waiting for her gangster boyfriend to fix his motor.

'Patrick?

'My brother. He wants to meet you.'

I shook my fist at the car. 'Bloody thing.'

She walked round to the driver's door and opened it. 'If we raise the bonnet it will cool down quicker. The front of the bonnet popped up as she released the catch. I propped it upright. Steam was rising from the radiator.

'Yeah, Patrick can sort this out later.' She was still standing there, her coat wrapped around her. 'Come on, I'm hungry.'

I took her by the hand as we walked into the pub. It was warm and cosy and smelt of the burning wood fire. We chose a table for two upon which had been set a red rose in a small vase. I touched one of the petals and discovered it was real.

Melanie removed her coat and then held my hand across the table. 'Tell me more, Mr Mysterio. What's the notebook all about? You're acting like a policeman writing down everything that happens.'

I laughed. The waitress brought menus and I was still

laughing. 'You know, it would be a relief to get all of this off my chest.'

We ordered drinks. Surprisingly, the pub offered cocktails so we both had margaritas.

'I'm still here,' she said, 'waiting.'

'OK.' I sighed and began to explain. 'It's a project I'm doing as part of my course. I study Fine Art, whatever that is. We all have to complete a project in our final year, on anything we like. They're pretty liberal on what counts as art.'

'You're a student at the university?'

'Yeah, but not the one you're thinking of. The smaller one, on the outskirts of the city.'

'I've still met a clever boy.' She took a sip from the frosted glass. 'I'm very simple, me. I left school at sixteen and I've worked on the farm ever since.'

I snorted, disparaging her humility. 'You're not in the slightest bit simple.'

'No, I've a great body and a great mind.'

'Agreed.'

We flashed shiny white teeth at one another and held hands again, fingers cold from clutching the margaritas.

'Will you tell me more about the project?'

It was less a question than a command. I suppose I always knew there would come a time when I would have to confess. I had thought it would be Nigel in the Haywain who would figure out what I was up to first. I had spent so much time perfecting my role of PI with Mick that I'd neglected to try to pull the wool over Nigel's eyes.

'I'm writing a short story about an artist. I have to write it in real time, even when driving. But you're right, that's both awkward and dangerous.'

Melanie was listening intently. Suddenly she produced my journal and wiped the mud and leaves off the cover. The smile slipped from my face. 'Just exactly what have you written in here?' She read the first few pages, playfully shrinking away from me every time I tried to take back the journal. When I finally got my hands on it she said: "Absolutely no nooky for you later on, Mister, if you don't let go.'

I relented. To be honest it was good to be finished with the damned thing. It had to be passed on to two academic examiners now. The future of my degree hung in the balance.

She read for a while as I drained my margarita. I reflected that I should have been drinking it on a beach in Florida. Still, you can't have everything.

'So, there's this good-looking artist and a private investigator is hired by his girlfriend's father to write a report about him.'

'Yes.'

'And the artist is called Alexander, so that's you. But I know you're the author. So you've actually written a book about yourself, from the viewpoint of the PI.'

'Boom.' I said the word quietly, plucking at and scattering a few rose petals across the table. The waitress had reappeared and was looking on admiringly.

We ordered roast beef with all the trimmings. I switched to drinking Coke. Melanie asked for a pint of lager. Her skin was radiant. She was enjoying my discomfort, sympathetically holding my hand but at the same time keeping firm control of the journal.

'This is how it works,' I said: "He sits at the table with the beautiful young woman. They hold hands across the table. It is evident that they are very much attracted to one another.

154

He is relaxed and happy, the first time I have truly him so. She listens to his account of his project, and his philosophy of life. The phrase brings a frown to her forehead which quickly subsides. He is an artist working on a project; as he explains, like much art it can be difficult to fathom at first."

She replied by placing a finger on my lips: "She stops him, with a finger on his lips. I get it; you're more both a writer and an actor. "

I replied: "He continues, flushed with excitement. That someone gets him is exciting. Although he will explain and clarify his position, just to be sure."

Melanie gave my hand a squeeze. 'It's OK. You're writing a book about yourself,' she said. 'You imagine you're sitting in the corner of this room and then you pretend a private investigator is watching us and then you write an account of it for your project. I get it.'

'Good. More than anything, an artist wants to be got.'

She said: 'I can see that he is pleased, because his shoulders have relaxed and he's happy to talk about something personal to him, which makes him the first one able to do that in quite a while.'

'It's self-reflexive,' I said.

She looked amused at my po-faced remark and then fell over sideways in her seat, laughing her head off, making the table wobble, spilling her drink.

'It is the ultimate self portrait of a person, of the artist, of the imagined self.'

Melanie was doubled up, writhing on her seat.

I said: "He is smiling, aping himself. I can see his eyes twinkling from where I am pretending to eat my own Sunday roast in the corner of the darkened room. His companion, the young woman, is either ill or having a hysterical fit."

Melanie eventually pulled herself together. "She met the young man in a country pub. From my hiding place in the corner of the restaurant I can see that they get on like a house on fire. They talk and laugh about something that the young man has done or is doing; it's difficult to make out from where I am sitting in the gloom, eating my lukewarm roast pork and soggy roast potatoes. It seems evident that they are attracted to one another. She leans in to listen to what he has to say."

'Bravo!' I said. 'You've got it! Now try and do it consistently, when people are about. You will need a notebook to record what you imagine you look like when you're doing it. It's easier to do at my house, where I have a video-recorder and goggles. Out in the field it takes a lot of effort.'

She put the journal in her coat pocket. I noted that it was the left-hand coat pocket, and that the top of the book protruded slightly. I would await my chance to surreptitiously lift it out. 'But why do it at all? What sort of a kick does it give you?'

'How would you describe yourself?'

That brought her up short. She looked down at her plate of undercooked beef and thought for a moment. I took a sip of my Coke.

'Good with animals and I don't mind hard work. Not smart at school stuff, which I found very boring, but I can read and think straight. Love my family. Always hope for the best.'

'Do you know who you are?'

She took a deep breath. 'My name is Melanie Tanner. I'm twenty-one and ready to take on the world.'

I shook my head. 'Do you really know who you are? Have you ever met yourself?'

'Every morning in the bathroom mirror, I say hello. Then I brush my teeth and go out and say hello to the cows.'

'Do you think it's funny that you've never seen yourself from outside? Not with a mirror, which inverts the image, but with your own eyes? Even on video you look like another person.'

'What's so important about looks?'

'A great many things are based on looks. I'm just saying that it's funny that of all the people in the world the most difficult person for each of us to understand is actually ourselves.'

She didn't reply.

I said: "The conversation subsides between them. For the first time their eyes do not meet; she looks away. He has said something that she does not like. I strain to hear from my secret location."

I leant across the table towards her now. 'Of course what I've done is unusual, what I'm doing, I should say, and I still haven't finished. Call it weird if you want. But I have a project to complete and I want it to be meaningful. Not just another portfolio of self-portraits or clever computer transformations of the face.'

'Is it all about looks?' she asked.

'No, it's all about the within and the without as viewed by the same person. It's important to have a control, so I am my own control. I know what I am like within and I can also see, with the help of technology, what I am like from without. After a while, I can see what I look like using my mind's eye, like Emerson's eye. I'm hoping it will all eventually add up to something important.'

The waitress came along and cleared our plates. There was a moment when I thought Melanie would decline dessert and we would just go home.

When the table was clear, only the rose petals remaining, I asked Melanie, 'Have you ever painted your own portrait?'

She brightened a bit and sat straight up in her seat. 'I once painted a field of cows for a competition at primary school.'

'Excellent! How would you go about painting your own portrait?'

She thought for a moment and then pulled her phone from her pocket. She held it at arm's length in front of her and took a selfie. Then she turned the phone around and showed me the screen. 'I would try and paint this.'

I took her phone. 'Let me check.' I held up the wooden block with the table number on it next to my cheek and snapped a selfie. The image was shown with the table number the right way around.

'Very good. Back in the day artists would sit in front of a mirror and paint their reflection. Earlier than that, people used looking pools to see what they looked like. Then some artists got so good at portraits, including their own, that they would paint what they looked like straight from memory. They would paint their mind's eye image of their portrait straight on to paper with no intermediary.'

'I could never do that.'

'That's the artists' thing; they can paint many different images from memory. Pianists can play concertos from memory. Expert chess players can remember all the games they've ever played. People get to be freakish at the highest level of ability.'

'Are you a freak?'

The waitress arrived with two sticky toffee puddings. These brought a smile to my face and to Melanie's. These smiles were very welcome, but there are smiles and there are smiles. Actors smile. Lovers smile. It doesn't have to mean you're happy. In fact a smile is very close to baring the teeth, a pre-aggressive act; a crocodile's smile. Or a smile is a grimace of discomfort, of showing that you are in pain and the other person should help or leave you. If I don't stop now there will be no more Melanie and no happy Alexander; and I'll be single again.

We ate the puddings and talked some more, but not about the project. While thus engaged we looked every now and then at a middle-aged man who was sitting at a corner table, and who had ordered the slow roast pork and potatoes. Eventually we burst out laughing and the poor man looked up at us, disconcerted. We went to pay the bill at the bar.

In the car park my car stood in silence, the engine not obviously damaged, so I closed the bonnet. Melanie had my journal in the pocket of her coat. She'd covered it with her hand. The project was nearly at an end; I really needed to take the journal back. I was fully prepared for the car not to start or for Melanie to prefer to take a taxi home to Granary Farm, or to call her brother and ask him to come and collect her. But the old rust bucket did start and I held open the passenger door for her and she got in, her coat neatly folded across her legs, my journal safe in her pocket. For one queasy moment I remembered that the ripped-up photograph of Penny was still in the glovebox.

We spent the afternoon wandering around a park near the centre of town, wading through drifts of leaves in yellow, orange and gold. Melanie lay down on the ground and held her arms and legs straight by her sides, clearing a space of leaves to make a leaf angel. Then she got up and we ran hand in hand, kicking through mounds of leaves, until, breathless, she stopped to sit down on a fallen tree trunk. I seized the chance to create some wild art and laid out eight long brown branches across a blanket of the colourful leaves, interspersing white cow's parsley in swirls throughout until my impromptu installation bore a resemblance to Pollock's Blue Poles.

'Come back to mine,' she said.

CHAPTER 18

THE FARMHOUSE WAS huge. It had thick walls and an elderly cat that did not want to be stroked. Melanie's bedroom was warm. There were pink roses in bloom on the wallpaper and my own full pink rose in the bed.

When we got up her mother served our breakfast: porridge, compote of plums, herby sausages, poached eggs.

'So you're a student at the university?' her mother asked as we sat in her farmhouse kitchen. She was apple-cheeked and clearly amazed at her daughter's taste.

I nodded as I drank the unspeakable coffee. The quality of the beverage spoiled an otherwise perfect moment: my victory, my breakthrough into the inner sanctum, to be taken in as one of their own.

Melanie's eldest brother, Patrick, came in, wearing a brown gilet and green wellington boots. He had obviously just walked through a part of the farm that oozed green mud; I didn't want to know its source.

'How's your car?' he asked.

I handed him the keys. 'No idea,' I said.

He collected a doorstep of a bacon sandwich from his mother and headed out. When he was almost out of my view, as he passed his sister, he put his free hand on his bicep and raised his arm in another victory salute. Melanie aimed at him a kick which scudded off the flag tiles.

Just before we were ready to go I broke all the rules and

took a look at myself in a mirror. There had been two in Melanie's bedroom, one set in the wardrobe door and one on a dresser. I avoided both, which was easy as then I had other things to do, but under the bright lights in the bathroom I took a deep breath and courageously peered into the mirror above the sink.

I had quite a shock which I tried to mitigate by opening my screwed up eyes very slowly. My first thought was that my nose was crooked and I wondered if I had broken it, imagining for a moment that Christos really had landed a punch on me during our altercation. When I had fully opened my eyes my hair felt wrong; it sat on my head like a wig. I raised my right hand to the right side of my head where I parted my hair and the guy in the mirror raised his left hand to the left side of his head where he parted his hair. I tried to shake the guy by the hand but our knuckles met on the surface of the cold glass.

'Lies,' I said quietly. 'We're all mugs. We don't even see ourselves properly.'

'You OK?' asked Melanie as she waited by the car.

I gave her a smile and a wink and continued thinking in the same vein as we drove off, the engine note noticeably quieter than yesterday. If the external image of self helped to form your conception of your own personality and the external image was incorrect what did this tell you about your own conscious self-awareness? Did it mean that we have a false view of self? Was that why people needed shrinks like my mother, to tell them what they are really like? Was that why we needed friends, to keep ourselves grounded in reality?

'Where to?' I asked once we were outside in the farmyard.

'Your choice, Romeo,' she said.

I took a deep breath. 'I think we should take a trip down the river. Find a boat somewhere.'

'Will we really be able to find one?'

'I reckon there must be one tied up along the bank. We can borrow it and then bring it back.'

She just laughed. 'I love these little whims you have.' She pointed out a left turn for me to take. 'They have a boat at the Fox, we can borrow that.'

'That's what I said.'

We stopped at the Fox and at the bar I enquired about the boat, impersonating a rich American. This amused Melanie although she was well known there and bound to be questioned about me later.

And thus it came about that I rowed the lovely Melanie down the river and we looked like a fine couple in a song or a children's tale. Rowing was much easier than punting. I recognised parts of the cold and glassy river from that long night out under the stars. We drifted by ducks coloured deep blue and grey; with a bit more sunshine it would have been perfect.

She snuggled into me as we sat in our cold boat and looked out across the water to the willows beyond. 'I remembered what you said about the eye.'

'Emerson? Oh yeah. He was the dude.'

'But do you really believe in the eye? I wasn't so sure after that night with Christos.'

'Emerson was a poet and an artist; he'd let people get there on their own, using their intuition. Christos thinks it's all science and history, like a bunch of facts, but it's not.'

'Yeah, he really didn't like what you said.'

'It wasn't me; it was my character.'

'It wasn't me, officer,' aped Melanie, 'it was my character.'

She stood up and stretched, and her top rose up to reveal a bare midriff. She yawned and laughed and the curtain fell over her belly button.

We drifted along again in search of a landing stage from where we could walk into town for some lunch. She cuddled up to me in the boat, together sharing our warmth.

'Am I the only one?' she asked.

'Of course.'

'What about all those other women you invited around to your house?'

'Who?' because I genuinely had forgotten.

'One was called Ruth, but I didn't get the names of the others. One was young, about my age, the other two were two much older.'

I sat up in the boat. 'Oh, yes. I remember. Yeah, that was awkward.' I remembered that day well enough because it had been one of the most difficult on the project. That was the day after the night with Ruth, and then Melanie turned up with all those others. Fiona, the silvery blonde with very long hair who wore a seventies jumpsuit, and was an art tutor at college: predatory would be the best way to describe her. Joan was the brunette with similarly long hair; she was a friend of Fiona's. Joan was an abstract artist who had once told me that what I was doing reminded her of Haight Ashbury back in the day; she was obviously still back there herself in more ways than one. Then there was Erica, the girl in the red dress, a sight for sore eyes: Eroica, obviously. She was a fellow student of mine, someone I had met at college. She was studying music; the word must have got out that I was looking for models.

'What happened that day? Were you shy? You only had

five girls to satisfy.' She poked me in the ribs, which made me skim a stroke off the surface of the water.

'Not shy at all! I was busy! I was getting used to being the PI at the garage and then suddenly you all turned up at the house and I had nowhere to go. If you'd seen me, you'd have asked questions: why was I wearing a suit, why did I have a beard, what was going on? And it would have spoiled the whole thing.' I looked at Melanie who had buried her head chin deep in her fur collar. 'Sorry. I know it was odd.'

She shook her head. 'I didn't know you then. It's fine. That's what you were like.'

More people were now appearing on the path beside the river. A boat crew swept past us, rowing in smooth, rhythmical strokes, their breath rising up in the November chill.

We stopped when we reached a weir: we had no clue how to get over or round it.

'Tie it up here,' said Melanie. 'I'll let the pub know and someone will come down for it.'

'Just like that?'

'Of course!'

We clambered out of the boat, kneeling on the wet grass on the riverbank, and walked across a field that gave way to a path across a meadow. I recognised that we had come to the outskirts of the Lammas Land.

We bought coffee and cake in the teashop that sold teapots. Then we carried on walking through the town, enjoying being a couple.

'I don't usually come to this part of town much,' she said. 'We normally drive into the shopping centre over there,' she waved her hand. 'We park up, buy what we need and then drive back home. This is much nicer.'

We walked past a new shopping arcade, its arches gilded, its walls plastered with advertisements for high-end retailers. When we approached the post office and the bank next door to it I had to laugh as I remembered trying to pull off that encounter with Yash.

Melanie was pleased to see that a shop selling fragrances was having a sale. 'I can get Mum her birthday present,' she said. We went into the shop, which sold hugely overpriced perfumes, and I rolled my eyes because perfume is not expensive to make. I helped her choose a perfume which was at least correctly mixed, blending a rose base with vanilla high notes. She also liked one which matched pomegranate with elderflower. I bought her a bottle of it. She was astonished.

'It's so expensive!' she said.

'What's money for?' I replied.

Outside the shop she placed her hands on my head and kissed me. Her sooty mascara had smudged around her eyes.

'You're tired,' I volunteered.

'Up at day break, milk the cows twice a day.' She yawned and the bags under her eyes deepened.

We got a bus back to the Fox. Melanie told the landlord where we'd left the rowboat and then we walked on down the lane to the farm.

'When you wrote that bit,' she said, 'you imagined yourself walking behind us, making notes as the PI?'

'Yes, that's right. That bit was easy. Travelling in the punt with you while imagining I was in a following punt talking with a chauffeur was much more difficult. When did you read that?'

'When you were asleep and snoring. I was up all night. I've never read so much in my life. But I skipped most of it until I made my entrance. You make me out to be gorgeous.'

'You are gorgeous.'

We were at the farm gate and kissed each other on the lips. 'I've got a busy week ahead. Vet's coming in. Oh, you'll need this.'

She reached into her coat pocket and pulled out my journal. 'Here you go.'

'Thanks. I can hand it in now. I'll do that tomorrow.'

'Is it finished? Aren't you halfway up that hill in the car, trying to drive and write at the same time? How does it all end?'

'This is how it ends.' I took the journal back; it was a relief to have it in my possession again. 'Some say art is never finished, that it's just a doorway into another world, and there is no need for closure. Then again, other people say they need closure.' I started walking off down the lane. 'I'll call you tomorrow. I'll get a cab from the Fox.'

'Cab?' she called after me.

'I'm a rich American hipster, remember?'

CHAPTER 19

THE NEXT DAY I went into college for the first time in a very long while. I had woken early and didn't bother to wash before I set off because I just wanted to get the whole business finished. I was wearing the same clothes I'd been wearing the day before. As I walked in to town the dew on the meadow grass was clinging to my boots.

I saw my seat of learning with fresh eyes. A lot of new building construction was under way and there were posters proclaiming how great the place was and how satisfied the students with their courses. I was late with my submission, even allowing for the extension, but who can rush art? was the question I had prepared to defend myself. A new academic year had begun. My contemporaries had all graduated but I believed that I would catch up with them.

The first person I met on this historic trip was Erica. She was emerging from the music department carrying a large chessboard. She saw me and stopped, then leaned back on the railings.

'Well if it isn't the artist himself, famous everywhere.'

'Hello Erica.' I clutched my journal in its brown padded envelope.

She looked me up and down and searched my face. Her hair was falling in waves as she shook her head.

'What you working on?' I asked.

'Oh, you'll like this.' She propped the chessboard up on the railing. 'It's musical chess. The chessboard plays a synthesised musical note for each move of a game. Do you want to hear it?'

'Of course!'

We went back inside and found a pod in a quiet corridor, comprised of a comfy chair and a table in front of a large square abstract painting of goodness knows what quale the artist was experiencing at the time. Erica set the board down and disappeared down the corridor. I turned the chess board over. There was a black circle under each square. Wires were leading from all the circles to a junction-box on the side of the board. Erica returned with the chess pieces and a speaker that she plugged into the junction-box. We set up the board; I took the white pieces and she the black ones. She pulled out a piece of paper on which was printed an account of the moves of a famous chess game, the so-called Evergreen game between Adolf Anderssen and Jean Dufresne. 'Can you read chess notation? OK, then follow this.'

I looked at the hieroglyphics and slid out the white king pawn two squares. A short synthesised note emerged from the speaker.

'It's only MIDI,' she said, 'but it's a start.' She moved the opposite black pawn, which played a note a fifth higher in the scale.

I responded; as we played out the moves I listened to the growing tension in the music. I played as Andersen, who set up pin after pin until, with a sense of escalation, the tide broke and white delivered mate with two bishops and an advanced pawn. It made a curious sort of sense. The music really did follow the moves; there was correlation, there was coherence.

'This is excellent,' I said.

Erica shrugged. 'It scored a B grade.'

'How you can score this sort of work?'

'They can,' she nodded, indicating the inside of the building. 'The examiner said it was pathetic, like the gloomy weather matching someone's gloomy thoughts.'

'Sympathetic would be better. Why don't you develop it for your final year project? It's got infinite possibilities; there are a lot of chess games out there. You could change the starting key or use modes, and see what music suits the game best.'

She brightened. 'That's a good idea.' She looked at me with that impish look which first made me invite her round to my place. 'How did your project go?'

'All done.' I patted the brown padded envelope. 'It's a written work based on self-reflection, critical self-awareness, that kind of shit.'

'You did that in your second year, didn't you?'

'And third year and now into part of my fourth year; I even had to pay more fees, at least my Father did.'

'I thought you were into videos, of yourself and others?' She frowned. 'Wasn't there some machine you made that would produce unconscious images? I came to offer to join in, but you didn't turn up.'

'Sorry. There was a lot going on that day. Yes, there were videos, then I had to narrate the videos and it took some time.'

She was looking at me, intently staring at the top of my head. 'Are you OK?'

'Totally.' I got up and moved along. 'I've got to get going and finally hand this in. You've got a great idea there, so make sure you don't give up on it.'

I passed by other groups of students. It struck me that we all looked similar. We all wore dark T shirts and donkey jackets and we were mostly young lads. We laughed and joked:

everything was a hoot. I eventually found the flight of stairs which led to the Students' Office. I wanted to offload my project. The secretary looked twice at me, slid the journal out of its envelope, made a note in a ledger and gave me a receipt.

I felt a mixture of relief and anti-climax. I was free! The rest of my life lay ahead of me. I wandered around the studio space where I used to work. I strolled past other studios with pink floors, some furnished only with a single wooden pallet. Other work spaces had large concrete slabs piled up like gravestones, artificial grass growing between the pieces. Saying goodbye was not an altogether pleasant feeling. The future loomed: a mighty big space to fill. I thought *The Book of Alexander* had looked quite insubstantial as it lay on the counter in the office. Some of the other students had submitted much larger installations.

I walked home, taking the route across the common. Passers-by looked up at me but made no attempt to speak to me. There's self-consciousness and there's self-awareness, the feeling of being watched. I'd never really experienced the latter before because I was doing the watching. But now I felt odd, exposed, scrutinised.

I reached home still with the sensation that I was being watched. How could this be? The project was over; I was unencumbered now. It was a depressing thought. I pined for Mel–an–ee. I wanted her. I sat on the chair in my study and looked out of the window, having raised the blinds, not caring who saw in. The garage was gone, reduced to dust. I stood to look sideways down the street. There was hardly anyone about any more. Outside presented a very blank and foreboding canvas.

I glimpsed something new in the reflection, even though

I had avoided looking at it directly. There was something on my forehead. When I reached up and touched it the tip of my finger was tinged with red lipstick. For the first time I had occasion to curse the lack of mirrors in the house and went downstairs in search of a reflective surface. Hitting on the side of the kettle, I managed to discern the distorted image of my forehead. It sported a red Hindu dot front and centre, painted there by my clever farmer's daughter.

Later my unconscious mind tossed out many memories and reminiscences. My forehead was now wiped clean. I luxuriated in the comfort of my sofa, cradling a mug of tea. I had failed the mirror test: I had proven myself to be unaware of my external appearance. Me! The expert on self-reflection: the artist and fearless investigator who recorded videos of himself for a deeper insight into his own character! The guy who had got so good at drawing his own portrait that he didn't need a mirror anymore, believing the sheer mental representation of himself to be enough. I had been quite unaware of that very berry-coloured lipstick dot planted on my brow by the devious Melanie. I was as ignorant of my own self as a gorilla or a gibbon in the jungle.

The next day was Thursday. I woke up laughing. I texted Melanie and suggested that we meet in town but she replied that there was extra work to do on the farm: cattle, vets, inoculations, something about a dairy inspection. Instead she agreed to a date on Friday night. I spent the rest of the day preoccupied with how to make it exciting.

The moment I woke up on Friday I texted Melanie. Seated at the kitchen table, I drank a cup of tea and listened to the workmen arrive with their grumbling diggers. I dressed, leaving the house by the back door, and wandered down to the river. My car was there, parked in the weeds, not quite immobilised by the undergrowth. The rusting bodywork told me it was on its way out. However, it started with just a single cough in protest.

I picked up Melanie at the farm gate. She had her hair scraped back into a ponytail looped high at the crown of her head. She wore larger earrings than usual. Her nail varnish sparkled. She was wearing a tracksuit top. Simultaneously she managed to look scrubbed clean and a little jaded: both her cheeks were peppered with acne.

'You look lovely,' I said.

'Whisk me away from all this. I've had enough of cows' backsides.'

We took a ride in a hot air balloon, something I had always wanted to do. We loved soaring above the town. Melanie looked down and pointed at the river wending its way past the conurbation and all the way to her house, that big farmhouse out on its own, lost in the back lanes. Our pilot then sailed with us above my house, near to which the ground was picked clean where the garage had once stood. Straight lines at right angles had appeared on the old forecourt, the foundations of future houses. The sun glinted off the river behind. I could make out the bridge over the river and the path that straddled the meadow. Mick had tumbled to my game on that bridge; Yash had already worked out what I was up to, which was why I avoided his shop now. But there's no law against exploring your surroundings and if I had duped anyone, although I was sorry, no harm had come of it.

We landed in a field. The pilot informed us we were three miles from where we had started. The pilot's wife was waiting to meet us in her Land Rover; she drove us back to Adelaide

Road. Then she went back to the landing site to help her husband prepare the balloon for the afternoon flight.

The rest of the day turned out very well. In the afternoon we made love in my room, Melanie careless whether the cameras were on or not. We relaxed into one another. It felt wonderful. By the early evening she was asleep in my bed. Later I slipped in next to her and felt like the luckiest man alive.

Daylight peeped through the blue blinds over the bedroom window. Outside was a new noise, made up of the notes of different engines. Two back-hoe loaders were extending the channels dug in the dirt. Workmen were standing in these channels holding sections of pipe. Something new was emerging: a sign erected at the side of the road informed us that the development was of luxury one- and two-bedroom apartments.

I brought Melanie a mug of hot chocolate when she awoke; after drinking it she got up and showered. We went downstairs to sit opposite one another at the kitchen table.

There were more questions. 'Who played the part of the 18th century gentleman?' she asked. 'And why did you dress up in the same way?'

'It was a friend from art school,' I lied. 'Everyone does it. My mate's an actor; he's very good, always up for something a bit different. We play parts all the time, hiding ourselves, outing ourselves.'

'OK. You like dressing up.' She frowned. 'And who were you at the Starlight? I can't remember what Christos said.'

'Christos? Forget him, the big wind bag.' A giant leaf, orange and yellow, glided past the window: an autumn romance now falling from its tree in bright yet fading colours to settle on the ground, eventually to turn to dust.

'I'd like to know, to try to understand. Otherwise you'll probably think I'm stupid.'

'I will never think you're stupid,' I said. 'It was just a lark. Remember, I had a girl to impress. I could have been anyone. I could have been a playwright called Goethe or a theologian called Feuerbach. Romantics, both of them, sceptical of the written word.'

'You wrote a lot of words,' she said.

'And I will soon have to answer for them, especially to my parents. They paid my fees, and this is their house. They love their darling son, but there will be problems if I haven't got a good grade.'

The hot chocolate wasn't pepping Melanie up at all. She still looked tired.

'There's a service with candles next Sunday, not tomorrow. Will you come to church?' she asked.

I took a long pull from my cup. Will you come to church? Not, shall we go together? More instances of the pathetic fallacy fell silently around my ears.

'Do you think I'd like it?'

She shrugged. 'I'm not sure, but I'd like to go.'

I shrugged back. 'Fine, I don't mind.'

Melanie left the table to pace round the kitchen. Then she sat down on the sofa near the fire and looked out of the window at the grey sky. Soon she got up and walked about again, then started playing with the pictures on the wall. Eventually she disappeared into the white room and stayed there.

I washed up the cups, devoting the time to some more thinking.

When I followed her into the studio Melanie was seated,

staring into the video camera. She stroked the velvet legs of the three-legged stool and sniffed the vanilla powder in the bowl and listened to the music. She rolled her eyes at the Spanish beauty. The software became confused and declared a fault. No image was printed to summarise her multisensory response so she assumed that my invention was not working, which vexed me greatly.

I turned off the video camera and stood behind it while she remained seated, looking at me. She had her right leg crossed over her left leg and her left arm was raised up at the elbow on her right arm, so that her left arm was supporting the left side of her face. She stared at me without blinking. I was very taken by the pose, the architecture of the way she had arranged herself, its semblance of concentrated study.

She was wearing blue jeans and brown boots and a blue-and-white striped top. She had now parted her hair in the middle. She was completely fixated on the video camera. I took a still shot, immediately displaying it on the white wall of my studio.

She unfolded her arms and legs and turned around to inspect it.

'I look well serious.'

'You look beautiful,' I said. 'Comfortable in your own body; that is something that cannot be faked.'

She came towards me and suddenly poked her tongue out at me: I saw it was the exact shape of a steam iron. It was hot when I took it into my mouth and then, magically, it cooled like an ice cream, getting cooler and cooler the longer it explored my mouth.

She had my cock out of my trousers in a second and it became a rifle in her hand. We backed up against the wall, both absorbed by the projection of her thoughtful face. I had no more time to think, only to do.

Afterwards, we walked, lazily, drunkenly, my arm draped over her shoulder, to the Hay Wain for lunch. She had pulled on my jeans and my shirt and borrowed a cowboy hat from the room upstairs, whose door I had forgotten to lock. I heard her rooting about in the dressing-up box and then registered the momentary silence when she discovered the cupboard of skulls. But she didn't even mention them, keeping on searching until she found what she wanted. She appeared, triumphant, holding a pair of sunglasses, their circular lenses encased in yellow frames.

I didn't know if she knew she had a patch of pox marks on her back: they raised her skin, making it look like small pieces of popcorn in the middle of her upper back. It was an area she would be unable to reach or see, the spots reminding me now of the nipples of her small breasts. I had read that butchers caught infections from cow skin, or was it pig skin, and supposed it was an occupational hazard encountered by farmers and their daughters. I then thought about my own meat and pigs' ears and purses and the life of microorganisms. And when we entered the Hay Wain it didn't just seem like the local pub, but a vibrant palace of colour where nothing was in focus but everything was experienced through the eyes. I was like Teucer: tall, lean, with oiled muscles, spearing women with arrows or swords or with the light from my eyes.

Nigel was experimenting with a new chef. Melanie and I both ordered the same pasta dish. It arrived in white oval bowls accompanied by a pot of parmesan with a small spoon. We devoured the little golden tubes, relishing the flecks of ham running through the dish.

'This is good,' I said. 'The olive oil and lemon echoes the prosciutto which echoes the thyme.'

Melanie looked at me. 'You're a funny one, aren't you, what with all the creeping about and costumes.'

Nigel came over and asked what we thought of the food.

'Sorry, mate,' I said. 'The food's good, but, no offence, it might be a bit too posh for around here. What happened to all the pies?

'Yeah, we've still got the pies for the builders.' Nigel gave a nod to the workers outside. 'But what do I do when they're gone, once they've put those smart new houses up? I need to diversify, that's what my accountant says.'

'Hence the posh grub.' I nodded approvingly. 'You're a busy man, Nigel. I'm just a humble plodder.'

Nigel laughed. 'You're what? You're PC Plod, now, are you?' He laughed again. 'You need to get a job, keep yourself busy.' As he cleared the table I could smell his bad breath.

CHAPTER 20

'I'LL SHOW YOU how to do it if you like.'

'Do what?' she asked from the bedroom.

'Act the part of the PI.'

There was silence for a long moment. 'OK. Do you have a hairdryer?'

I surely had one somewhere. I found it next door in the room that I usually kept locked. The hairdryer, covered in paint from experimental use in drying papier mâché, was at the bottom of the cupboard where I kept the human skulls (they offered excellent practice when portrait drawing).

Melanie, now clean and fragrant, sat next to me, sharing my chair at the desk. We looked out at the street. 'There's two ways of doing it. First way is to throw your imagination into a distant spot and then look back as if you were viewing from that place. Then write what you imagine you see.'

'Like we did in the pub?'

'Exactly; you were a natural.'

She squirmed. 'OK. You write down what I say. My writing is bad.' She shook her head, making her newly washed hair, not quite dry at the ends, flick across my face.

She said: "I'm hidden in the remains of the office. The workmen don't bother me. They think I might be policemen or from the tax office or customs and they leave me alone. Mick has been crying, he's so upset at losing this place."

'Crying?' I ask.

'Yeah, he's well upset.'

'Go on.' I giggled.

"There's not much going on at Alexander's house. Earlier on there was some movement behind the blinds, as if someone was getting out of bed. But nothing else happened; whoever it was might still be sleeping, for all I know."

Melanie watched me finish writing this down. 'How's that?'

'Brilliant. One thing to add: Alexander made breakfast in the kitchen and turned on the light, which you can see from outside. So you could add that in.'

'Yeah, let's do that.'

I add in a couple of sentences but I can tell Melanie is losing interest. I read the paragraph aloud and put down the pen.

'Not much happened,' she said.

'True, sometimes it's just run-of-the-mill, nothing much happens, that's just life.'

In fact, it's lunch-time. I'm starving and she must be starving, too. But we need something to divert us before yet another pub meal. Either that, or to have sex again.

'The second way of doing this is to actually go there and take on the persona of the third eye, in this case the private investigator. Then you write what you really see, because you really are watching my house and this window. But you can also add in details of what you reckon Alexander and friends would actually be doing or what they have just done.'

She stood up and found her fur-lined parka under the bed. 'Come on then, let's do it. Then buy me lunch, I could eat a horse.'

I grinned. 'This is great. I'll introduce you to Mick.' I

looked her up and down. 'You could be a member of the public who has come forward with some information about Alexander. '

'What information? What do you want me to say?'

'I told Mick that Alexander might be a computer hacker. Let's say Alexander contacted you online with some dodgy idea, and you found out where he lived.'

'What dodgy idea?' There was a great roar outside as a bulldozer, now near the road, knocked flat the remaining wall.

'I don't know. You can improvise; that's half the fun.'

In the dressing room I changed into a two-piece suit, also selecting a woollen square-cut tie. I stuck the beard back on without looking in a mirror, although I asked Melanie to inspect my efforts. I saw she'd discovered the blue frock coat, buff leather waistcoat and breeches which were hanging in the wardrobe, but she didn't mention it.

Downstairs again, I pulled on a pair of brown tasselled loafers that I always kept in the box they'd been bought in. Melanie just wore her usual clothes. 'You look great,' she said, 'young and trendy. Love the shoes.' She paced about, clearly searching for something. 'You don't actually have a mirror in this place, do you?'

'I can tell you that you look lovely.'

'But would it be true?'

I slipped on my shoes. 'Why don't you tell me what you look like?'

'Like a dancer in a band on a break from a TV show.'

I unlocked the back door. 'Now we're getting somewhere, getting close to the real you.'

'That's just a fantasy!

We walked down the garden path side by side. The

fountain was silent although the pump was switched on. The peacock looked at us with its many eyes.

'Fantasy one day, reality tomorrow; the moral is not to hold back your dreams.' We left through the garden gate and crossed the road to walk alongside the river. I placed my hand on the bonnet of the car as if it was an old pet.

'Where are we going?' asked Melanie.

'We're going the long way round to the garage. Remember, I am not Alexander, so I can't be seen coming out of the front door of his house.'

Walkers with dogs and cyclists heading for the bridge passed us by. We turned left up the street, heading towards the Hay Wain. There were some people about and a few parked cars. I had my notebook with me. Walking by my side was a young woman I had recently discovered snooping around Alexander's house.

I explained as much to Mick when I met him sitting in his car behind the remains of his office and shop. 'This is Melania,' I told him. Melanie didn't bat an eyelid at the change in pronunciation of her name. 'She has agreed to help me with my investigation.'

'You again,' said Mick, whom I was a bit wary of meeting, but he was smiling. 'How do you know our friend?' he asked Melanie.

Melanie looked confused.

'Her English isn't so good,' I explained. 'She's a dancer in a nightclub.'

Mick looked at Melanie again.

'Our target was in the club. He was drunk and getting a bit vocal about some scam he'd pulled off at a bank. Trouble is, Melania had an account there and was terrified she'd lost her money. So she followed him home. I saw her hovering about and she's agreed to help me by showing me where he likes to hang out.'

I screwed up my eyes as I spoke: even in the weak November sunshine the light reflecting off the chalky white land where the garage had once stood glared unpleasantly. Melanie wrote in the notebook, I hoped neatly, because that journal had taken a lot of time and effort.

Mick looked at me, then at Melanie again, and I'm sure he was about to say that he wasn't that stupid when his mobile went off. Mick was immediately deep in conversation with the caller. We walked away, Melanie still scribbling.

'I don't think we can stay here for long,' I told her. 'Get what you can in the way of images of the house and the bedroom windows and then we'll disappear.'

'No joking,' she replied. 'You look too young to be doing this sort of thing and your beard is peeling off.'

Melanie walked past the builders. They were busy directing the digging of the foundations; no fewer than four backhoe loaders were tracing the rectangular bases of the houses of the future. I walked past my house, took a long sideways glance at the blue front door, and smiled.

The contact of metal on concrete as a pneumatic drill pierced it made me jump. The men laughed; I laughed too. Melanie walked past six builders who were sitting on a wall. Each either nonchalantly rolled a cigarette or sent his eyes heavenward as she passed. She flipped them the bird as they called to her in another language. They were almost cheering.

Melanie was right. I could feel the beard lifting away from my skin. You can only stick and reapply false beards a certain number of times.

We walked away, keeping going until we'd gone a mile or so out of our way. Finally we flopped down on a bench, our arms entwined.

'Can I see what you wrote? Or do you want to read it to me?'

'You can read it if you like.'

It took me a while to get used to the scrawl.

I read: "When are you coming home, darling? You work so hard and our son misses you. This case is beginning to take you over. I don't even know who you are any more. You need a break. We all need a break together. The travel agent phoned today and offered an all-inclusive break in Florida that sounded wonderful. Jonty is so excited. He's told all his friends at school that he's going to America with his Mum and Dad on holiday at Christmas. Let's book it now and leave this place behind."

'Jonty?'

'Poshest name I could think of.'

The wooden bench was cold and wet. My trousers were getting progressively wetter. I felt none of my former hot passion. Winter was on its way.

'Did you actually pay yourself for the work?'

'No, I went to the post office and pretended it was the bank.' I brightened a little bit. 'That was fun, pretending in front of so many people was a real blast. But then I saw someone I knew and I bottled it.'

'Who hired you do to this job? Who was it really?'

I turned to her and saw that she'd found the one dry spot on the bench. 'Self-reflexion,' I said. 'Look it up.'

She ignored my tone. 'OK, so answer this one truthfully. Are you really seeing a therapist?'

'I can quite honestly say that I've seen a therapist all my life.' My voice was grave although I was play-acting.

'Oh.' She was silent for a while. I sneaked a glance at her and saw that she looked perturbed.

'It's my mother. She is a genuine therapist, a psychoanalyst.' She became even more concerned.

'My mother is a therapist. My father is an artist. If you add the two together you get me.' I stood up, wet suit trousers clinging to skin. 'You should meet them. They'd love to meet you.'

Melanie went back to the farm that evening. It was her Mum's birthday on the next day, strictly a family affair. We hugged and kissed goodbye, then I drove her home. As I waved goodbye at the gate I hoped I would see her again.

CHAPTER 21

In less than a week my examiners had read my submission. They'd really gone to town on it judging from the numerous coloured sticky notes that poked out from between the pages of the journal. I was pleased they had bothered to be so thorough. I only needed a pass to graduate; I cared nothing for the class of degree they decided to award to me. Father was hoping for a First, of course; Mother was barely interested. 'Do you think an arbitrary value can ever reflect the true nature of your work?' she had asked. She was always right, just as Father was always innovative and thinking ahead of the curve. It was best merely to achieve something, finish it and then defend it, as I had in my viva.

The internal examiner put me at my ease. I was told that the project work was good, and that he and his colleague wanted only to clarify a few points. They had never before encountered anything like my thrown third eye writing perspective. They said I would be likely to receive high marks. I said that my father would be happy. They asked me if I would be happy. I replied that I hadn't started on the project to get marks: I'd done it because I hadn't known myself.

I thought it was cold in the room. I was wearing only a shirt and I started to shiver, so I put on my jacket. The examiners were both in shirt sleeves. The heating was turned up high. I wondered if they thought I was nervous, or worse, cracking up under the strain.

What had I learnt about myself, they asked, from the innovative line of enquiry I had taken? Had I now managed to see myself clearly, no pun intended?

I told them what I had learnt about my physical appearance as observed from the outside. I had looked sterner, tougher, more chiselled than I expected. My face was more slab-like. My eyes blinked a lot, like antennae, like eyeballs on stalks connected to the brain. The examiners agreed that my banishing mirrors from my house was not particularly abnormal. I said that the absence of mirrors in the house and consciously avoiding them when I was outside the house had helped with the video experiments. I had a better sense of me as another person when I was the observer. I realised I had started to match my internal feelings with a better external view of myself. I thought it was funny that I looked perplexed when I had been thinking great thoughts. I knew that I could not determine what I was thinking from merely looking at myself, not even in the videos in which I could remember what I had been thinking. I concluded that other people were just the same as I was and not philosophical zombies. I had got precisely nowhere with the great question of consciousness, but I realised with a sudden brightening of spirit and straightening of my back that I was now more content with just being me.

My examiners liked that.

I suggested that I had found a new way of telling the mundane story of our lives.

The external examiner liked the idea of exploring the mundane from a young person's viewpoint. 'We see so much yearning and striving to be original,' she said, 'it's refreshing to see the mundane.'

It all got a bit serious when I said that I needed to flee the head of Medusa and get away from life under my own gaze. I said that such a laser-like vision could be damaging to some relationships and that it might turn other people to stone.

There was some sympathy in my examiners' faces. The internal examiner, whom I remembered was also responsible for pastoral support at the university, asked me what I planned to do next. I told him that I would take a break, perhaps visit certain art museums in Norway that interested me. They, too, were aware of these places, and commended me on my choice.

My examiners asked me to leave the room for a few minutes while they had a brief discussion. I had already sensed that everything was going to be OK. They didn't keep me waiting for long: soon I was back in the room, listening as the internal examiner announced that I had passed the project. I had been accepted as being normal after having done an extraordinary thing, an interesting dichotomy that I would look forward to batting around with Mother and Father.

But I needed to get away. Shed off some skin. Come back transformed.

Once we were outside in the corridor and he had said goodbye to the external examiner, the internal examiner took me aside and said that I had done well enough but he wasn't allowed to reveal how well. University regulations had to be applied: the work had been handed in late and therefore a penalty must be applied before the class of degree could be decided.

I reminded him of a story about Salvador Dali, who had contended that having examiners to mark work of a creative nature was very difficult. (I resisted saying impossible or ridiculous.) We're not all Salvador Dali, said the examiner.

As I left the building the town had never looked so good: I finally felt that I belonged there. I passed the statue of the king with an orb in one hand and a chair leg in the other. A cheese shop captured my attention and then a lingerie shop; passing it, I thought about Melanie and then I passed a gentleman's outfitters, where I thought about graduation and Melanie and Mother and Father all mixed up in a fantasy of the future.

I went to sit in the market café again, this time taking a table inside the building. I enjoyed my espresso, glad to be able to escape the gaze of all those inscrutable buildings. I had finished my project and I felt proud. What might happen next I had no idea, but I knew a doorway had opened. My journal was to be digitised and the original returned to me. The electronic copy would be made available to other students looking for a good example of project work. In the meantime I had pressing things to do. I needed to scrap Father's old car before it died on the road with me in it. I needed to retrieve that old ripped-up and stuck-back-together photo of Penny from the glovebox before Melanie saw it. I really should return Nabokov's autobiography to the library but I had scribbled in it so much I decided I would keep it as a memento and pay the fine.

I walked home across the common, pleased not to have to write down everything I was doing in my book. Even so, I couldn't resist one more experiment with the thrown third eye view, if only for old time's sake.

I watched Alexander as he walked up to his front door. He seemed to be in good spirits, walking quickly, hands in his coat pockets, chin tucked in to his scarf, not minding the autumn leaves that swirled around his feet. When he reached the doorstep of his house he looked across the road at the spot where the garage had stood and took in the transformation. Grey rubble was neatly piled in heaps, leaving some areas clear. I stood behind one of the diggers and was now out of his range of sight. I could feel his eye on me and didn't doubt that he knew I was there.

Sleep came very easily. The postman arrived in the morning with a letter from the university. I went upstairs to read the letter while I sat at my desk. The letter informed me that I had passed my final assessment and that I would be awarded an Upper Second in Fine Art from the not quite as prestigious university as its famous counterpart in this famous university city.

I then wrote a letter to Mother and Father to tell them the news. Yash was surprised to see me when I went into the post office for stamps. 'Shame about Mick and the garage closing,' I said.

'Yeah, he was very upset, and Ying too.'

'Nice people,' I said. 'I hope they'll be OK.'

I placed the letter in the post box, returned home, and hoovered the house from top to bottom. I would expunge that last project from my life and start afresh on something new. Melanie texted when I was midway through this cathartic activity, sending her congratulations. She said she couldn't get away from the farm to celebrate until the weekend: bloody cows, literally.

Mother's letter arrived on Thursday. 'Well done, dear, we're terribly proud of you. We shall have a celebration. Come over to the house on Saturday for lunch and bring Melanie, won't you?'

CHAPTER 22

T HE FRONT DOOR of my parents' house was, of course, open. Even at their leafy end-of-avenue dwelling there was still reason for ne'er-do-wells to have a look through the big bright windows and think about walking in. I peeked behind Mother's hand-printed curtains featuring African scenes and saw within the front room many potted plants and the rubber tree with its long thick glossy leaves. There was no TV or stereo to nick; where they might have stood in other houses they had been replaced by a surround of low bookcases and abstract art on the wall. Maybe this stuff was worth a second look. It was the living room of the cognoscenti, the comfortably well off, even though in the driveway was a 2CV, and you'd need a knowledgeable fence to get rid of the Cubistes, the Dada and the Art nègre.

Inside, they were both relaxing. Mother wore a man's shirt, thick green stripes on white like the covering on a deckchair. She was indeed sitting in a green and white striped armchair: the whole effect may have been intended as one of her performance jokes. She was staring into space while listening to Father who, while lying prone on the brown sofa, was reading aloud from a book, his head resting on crushed cushions. He looked comfortable in a warm Norwegian sweater with blue and white spots. He was laughing but agreeing, I think, with whatever it was he was reading. He still had on his shoes. Perhaps Mother was thinking about that, because I knew she hated the way he kept his shoes on around the house.

I'd already told Melanie to slip off her pumps – they were more like school plimsolls – and I'd pulled off my brown brogues.

Mother looked up at us, then away again. We stood and waited. Father continued reading the passage, which was about Hans Hofmann, an American artist who set up schools for painters based on a new theory of Cubism and the vivid colour of the Fauves.

We stood there respectfully waiting to speak until he had finished. Then Mother got up and welcomed us in. I saw that she'd again had her hair cut in a man's style.

I got a dry brush on the cheek and smelt something new, a high note, a whiff of gin.

Melanie received a firm handshake. 'Hello, dear,' said Mother, as she stood holding on to Melanie's hand for a few seconds.

'Hello, Mrs Clearly,' said Melanie. 'I love the way your house looks.'

Mother smiled a wan smile. The bowl of fruit on the table looked tired: they never ate any of it. Father hid paper bags of sweets around the house.

Father stood up, his heels clicking on the wood floor.

'Come through to the studio,' he said.

We followed him, me first, then Melanie, then Mother. When their backs were turned I made the prearranged signal to Melanie, a T made with two hands as if I were a basketball coach. Father always carried out this exercise with whomever I brought home, male, female, young, old. The T didn't stand for Time out; it stood for Test.

The studio was a converted conservatory. Most of the windows had been covered with white muslin sheets, which Father liked to think softened the light. A bench and a chair had been pressed into duty as tables. On them he had placed the long wooden boxes containing his brushes and oils. There were potted plants on the floor placed well away from where he would be standing when at his wooden easel. This easel was a giant totem pole, a massive phallus that designated Father as the boss. As I had grown older and taller I competed with the easel until the top of my head reached the tip of it.

Father slackened the cord between the legs of the easel. Melanie was checking the health of the plants nearest her, the back of her hand surreptitiously touching the dry soil.

'What do you think?' Father asked Melanie as he stood in front of the empty easel.

'About these?' she said, indicating four pots of lifeless foliage, 'Soak the pots in a tray of water until the tops are wet, and give a shot of tomato feed. See if that perks them up.'

She twirled the end of a thick strand of hair in her fingers and walked over to the windows. 'You're growing mushrooms in here.' There were indeed white fungi sprouting under the muslin near the windows. 'They like the damp but would grow better in the dark.'

Father smiled. 'Observant.' He placed a small picture on the easel. It was a portrait of Mother with no clothes on, drawn from behind. In the picture Mother stood with her hands placed behind her head, looking away from the artist, her husband. I had got used to these portraits over the years. Only once did Father ask if I had wanted to draw one, to which I had answered in the negative.

'You look great in that,' said Melanie enthusiastically to

193

Mother. 'You could do one of those naked calendars and make some money.'

'I'm often tempted,' replied Mother, 'but Joseph would get jealous, wouldn't you, dear?'

Father nodded. 'I would, there's no denying it.' From a wooden cupboard he pulled out a small elephant made of clay and glazed green. 'Alexander made this when he was five.' He handed it to Melanie. 'I knew he was a chip off the old block from that day forth.'

'He's more into writing books now,' Melanie revealed.

'Gone over to the other side, have we?' Father folded up the easel and packed it away, just to make the point that he could still manage to do it all. I know it's a continuation of life for him, as is drawing Mother's behind as if she was still twenty-five.

'Let's eat,' interjected Mother. 'I have steaming bowls of kasha for us all, with mushrooms, and a pumpkin from the garden.'

Melanie took it all in her stride. 'I'll try anything once,' she said, as she followed Mother out of the room.

'Never a truer word said,' commented Father as he ushered me along the corridor to the dining room.

Over lunch my achievement was commented on very briefly. Father made a joke about me being allowed to remain in the house rent free as if it was some kind of graduation gift. Mother also found a way to talk to me alone. 'I've talked with Dr Ling and he says that you can stop yanking his chain now. You confabulate as well as any patient he's ever known, but you're no Walter Mitty.'

When we left in the car I could tell Melanie was glad to get away. 'Wow, your Dad is something else.'

'Father. Never once have I called him Dad.'

'Figures.' She blew out her cheeks, thankful for fresh air and the sky above. 'And there are no mirrors!'

'Really? What? No mirrors anywhere?'

'None. Not even in the bathroom, or the toilet, or in the hallway.'

'I'd never noticed before.'

'There are no mirrors in your house either. Why is that?'

'Well, if you must know, it's because we're a family of vampires. If we look in mirrors we turn into stone.'

She slapped my hand. Earlier on in our relationship it would have been a playful slap. This slap, however, stung the skin.

'No mirrors, because, why?'

I bit my lip rather than correct the syntax. 'We've never had mirrors. I think Father bought one once, for the hallway, but Mother took it down. She said if you break a mirror that means seven years' bad luck.'

'Rubbish,' said Melanie. 'You don't like mirrors because they don't show the real you.'

'Well, yes, that's right, to be honest. It's one of those funny things about life that no one comments on, but it makes my point. You never get to see your true self with your own eyes.' I can get quite excited about this concept so I consciously slowed down. 'I will never see my face as you see my face. I can see reflections and photographic images, videos and even selfies, but I will not get to see my face directly from my own eyes with nothing in the way. I've never seen my face in person.'

I had parked the car behind number 44, rolled back in the weeds as usual. These were now dying off so that an ominously large oil patch was becoming visible where they had been growing. Melanie still wanted to take me to task about mirrors and the lack of them, so I shushed her and crept up to the back wall.

'OK, this is our vantage point.'

Melanie crouched down next to me. People behind us walking dogs headed for the bridge. 'What are we doing?'

'We are playing the part of the PI again. We pretend we're watching our selves – yes, we speculate on what we are up to – it's self-reflection; Buddha would be proud.'

I peeped over the wall. 'OK, now because we're a bit nearer you can add in what might be heard from the house and any other detail from up close.'

'Do you do this with all your girlfriends?'

'No, you're the first.'

'Because I found your book?'

'Shush.' I looked over the wall. "I can see from my vantage point that Melanie is in the white room, his studio. I can see the top of her head through the window. She must be sitting on that strange stool, the one with the furry legs."

I noticed that Melanie had stood up.

'Get down or they will see us.'

'Sweetheart,' she said, 'do not ever shush me. No one shushes me, not twice in one day, not even to play a kid's game.' She stalked up the garden path and stood at the back door. I produced the key and let her in.

The temperature was somewhat glacial in the house even though the heating was on. 'Sorry,' I said. 'I should learn when to stop.' I switched on the kettle and washed out the teapot.

She didn't take off her coat as she sat down on the sofa. 'What have you learnt from your project?' she asked.

'That I'm a bit weird?' I offered.

She didn't say anything. I brewed the tea, brought her a cup and sat down at the kitchen table. It was as if I was talking to myself again. 'It is strange what I do, and how I do it, but I am tackling the toughest question of all, the hard problem, the mystery of consciousness. No one has a single clue as to what consciousness is and I think it's because we tackle it like we do a brick wall; we're trying to knock it down and pick up the pieces. Instead, we need to find the most different and alien way of looking at ourselves to try and get a handle on the problem, because it really is the most difficult and alien problem we have, and this is the solution I've come up with.'

'I don't think my Mum and Dad would be impressed.'

'Do you think animals are conscious?

'What? Cattle? Are you joking? Milk- and meat-making machines. The dogs are smart, and really loyal, but do they know what they're doing in the scheme of things? I doubt it.'

I was about to pick up on this when she asked simply: 'Can you be normal?'

'For how long?' I joked.

'Just while I'm here. Like when we were at the fireworks, I loved that, and the punting.'

'I wrote about that from without, I mean as the PI.'

'I know; it was nice.'

'I remembered a lot of it.'

'Was it memory or invention?

'That's a really good question.'

'Oh yeah, that writer guy, Nabokov – and I'm a butterfly, that's sweet, but it would be nice just to be a couple doing normal things and not go about investigating ourselves like you really are a policeman.'

We finish our tea in silence.

'Do you want to go out?' I asked.

'And follow ourselves to a wine bar?'

'Where the PI watched from inside, then legged it out the door, and waited at a bus stop?' I continued. 'No, not if you don't want to.'

For a while we were silent again. I knew that Mother would not have experienced such a problem with a lover: for her it all depended on the art of conversation.

'I would like to go out,' said Melanie, finally. 'Somewhere new; not a pub, or restaurant, or club, or gig, but something I haven't done before. Like that balloon ride, which was amazing.'

'You're very demanding.'

'Am I?' She looked a little worried.

I moved closer to her, sitting on the edge of the sofa. 'You make me smarten up my game, that's all. Luckily, I know just the thing.' I reached into my jacket and pulled out a flyer. 'There's an exhibition in town, it's on tonight.' I looked at the details. 'It's at a very posh gallery. Smart dress is called for.'

Slowly the smile grew on her face. 'Brilliant,' she said, and kissed me on the lips, then ran upstairs to the dressing room.

CHAPTER 23

MELANIE SCRUBBED UP nicely. She was wearing a black coat I remembered from a few years back. She looked smart. She'd put her hair up, which made her look older and more elegant. The walls of the gallery were white, as always. Everyone there was well dressed, over-dressed if I'm honest. Everyone was engaged in earnest conversation. No one was looking at the paintings, no one ever did. Inspection smacked of amateurship, of trying to understand, and in any case we were not there to judge. This was an opening show; we were all there to support the artist who had finally managed to get a platform for his work.

More people kept turning up: the artist was evidently popular, and after a while we felt a bit squashed in. Melanie and I were being nudged closer to a middle-aged woman who was talking to an older man. He might well have been the gallery owner. Melanie wilted a little as people ignored us and the temperature in the room rose. I smiled at her and put my arm around her. 'It's always like this,' I said, 'I'm just a student so I will be ignored, too.'

'Why?'

'Until you've exhibited, you're nothing.'

I recognised Joan, the brunette. She looked ravishing in a long-coated trouser suit, but I turned my back on her because I didn't want her to come and quiz me about my work. I took

Melanie's hand and we pushed our way outside. We walked down the set of steps that led to the main entrance of the gallery. High up on the corresponding flight, which led to the rear of the gallery, three men stood speaking in whispers. Two of them were grasping but not wearing their overcoats; the third man sported a blazer and tie. Down on the street we could see another man. He was wearing a jacket with large lapels and indigo denim jeans with big turn-ups and pacing about with his hands in his pockets.

Melanie pointed at him. 'Isn't that Christos?'

'Yes, it's his show.' I said. 'He's exhibiting under his real name, Nikos Dante.'

'I remember the night that you fought with him. You were funny and brave. He really doesn't like you, does he?'

'Yeah, you're right, we've sparred for years. It's taken him ten years to finish his degree. He did it part time while he ran the bookshop.'

'He said that you went to the Starlight when you needed love and support and now you've got them you've turned your back on it.'

'Like I said, we've sparred for years.'

'He looks happy now. Good for him: he's achieved his success. You're not jealous, are you?'

'I'm actually surprised to see him smiling. I hope he's OK.'

We walked on a while. 'Why do you say that?'

'Rumour has it that he tried to top himself once. Fell from a very high building, but somehow survived the fall. The paramedics got to him quickly and revived him.'

Melanie put her hand up to her mouth. 'That's awful.'

'Comes with the territory; it goes with the artistic temperament.'

'You'd never do that would you? What a waste that would be!'

'No, I'm all right. Mother says so.'

'Jesus.'

'I've lost sight of him.'

I led Melanie down the steps and away from the gallery. 'I take it you've had enough.'

'God, yes. Please, take me home.'

We walked on purposefully, intent on getting back as soon as possible, but as we passed through the market square Melanie decided that she wanted a hot drink. We ordered two hot chocolates in one of the cafés and took them outside because the crowd of loud-voiced business men inside had distressed Melanie with the noise they were making. I was happy to brave the evening chill myself because I had recognised a handbag, big and square and glossy in blue and black, hanging over the back of a tall chair in the cafe.

Melanie found a table but it had a wobbly leg so I looked about for a more stable one. The café had floor to ceiling windows: from its size and position I thought it might previously have been a bank. During my search for a decent table I became aware of my reflection flitting across the windows, trying to attract my attention. It was extremely difficult to avoid the liar and fool smirking in the glass, but I did so, even though Melanie kept waving over my shoulder at him.

'Cut it out,' I said, 'I'm not looking at that guy. He's a doppelgänger in two dimensions and not to be trusted.'

'It's not all about you, darling,'

Having an ex join you and your present flame for drinks is guaranteed to put you off your cocoa.

The young woman who had sat down at the original table Melanie had found looked corporate. She was dressed ahead of the season in a black jacket and short skirt surely not warm enough for the weather. She had fabulous legs: I remembered them well.

'Hello, Ruth, how are you?' I asked. 'Would you like a drink?'

She shook her head but did not look at me. 'No, thanks; I have a date. I just came out to get some air.'

I dragged another table across, its iron legs making a nasty screech on the concrete slabs. We sat together, Ruth and Melanie at their table, and me on my own at the other. Melanie seemed to be very pleased with this arrangement.

'We've met before, I'm sure we have,' said Ruth to Melanie. 'Of course, at Xandy's house, I remember it now.'

'That was quite a day,' said Melanie. 'The day he got lost.'

'Put not your trust in princes,' smiled Ruth.

'Nor in the son of man, in whom there is no help.' I responded.

When I had been inside ordering at the counter I had noticed a large advertisement promoting the café lifestyle, albeit in another country and climate. Two very attractive young women with model good-looks were seated at a table, talking to an equally attractive young man sitting at another table. From the width and brilliance of their smiles they could have been advertising dental services. The two young women were obviously thick as thieves; the young man, turned by their behaviour into a bit of an outsider, was forced to laugh along with them.

And so it was with us. Ruth and Melanie chatted about the day they had first met. Melanie remembered playing with the goggles and what a funny experience it had been to look at yourself using a bird's eye view.

I started a half-hearted explanation about my project, but Ruth waved it away. 'We are your project, Alexander Clearly.'

'How did the sparklers go down?' I asked.

'I managed to pass that idea on to a junior colleague and the project got killed. As was only right.'

An older man emerged from the café and offered his arm to Ruth. 'Shall we go?'

'Nice to meet you again, Melanie.' The two women air-kissed and Ruth walked away with the man, her lovely calves flexing under her milky skin.

I maintained a short silence, which I considered to be appropriate. A conversational gambit then occurred to me: 'At least I didn't get a friend to shoot me in the arm to make a split-second sculpture.'

'Sorry?' Melanie was peering with a certain displeasure that was perhaps directed at me, perhaps at the chocolatey bits at the bottom of her cup.

'It's a joke. About what some artists are prepared to do to be original.' I carried on. 'I've known artists willing to film themselves doing chores around the house.'

'Have you done that?'

'For a while.'

'Did what's-her-face like it?'

'What's-her-face?'

'The one before Ruth, the one you wrote about at the beginning of your journal.'

A radio was playing from somewhere across the market square. It took me ten seconds to tune into the language, which at first I thought must be Dutch but turned out to be

German, and it became clear to me that my brain circuitry had just figured that out for me. Somewhere in that three-pound lump of warm grey blancmange I had neuronal circuitry that responded to audio stimulation in a certain way; and, quite without any help from me, translated a stream of individual words in what we call a language.

It also occurred to me that consciousness was automatically the mind / body problem, and dualism was the default.

'Yeah, her name was Penny. But it wasn't the cameras. She knew what she was getting in to.'

'So what was it?'

I got up; the market square seemed smaller, just as well-known places from your childhood do when you see them as an adult.

'Come home with me and I'll show you.'

CHAPTER 24

W E DIDN'T JUST rush into it. I knew from experience that this latest exercise, which I originally learnt about in my second year at college, could test relationships to the limit.

As a prelude, I cooked the last chicken and ham pie with chips from the freezer, and found a tin of baked beans. After the meal, which Nigel would have laughed at, we sat on the sofa together and speculated about how to fix the fountain and whether the peacock would be better off moved to another position, perhaps high up on a perch.

Finally, Melanie could wait no longer. 'Do I have to take my kit off?'

'No! That comes later.' Although I doubted that would come later. With Penny, what had come later after she had agreed to this interesting but intense activity was, first, a cessation of love-making and, second, withdrawal and removal from the entire relationship.

We entered the white room. I sat on the stool and asked Melanie to stand behind the laptop.

'OK, sit down now, but turn sideways so you can see the laptop screen'

'Yeah, OK.'

I adjusted myself on the velvet-legged stool. 'OK. I can see myself on the video monitor. Can you see the image on the laptop screen?'

Melanie nodded. 'Yes, I can see you on the laptop.'

'And I can see myself on the video camera monitor, although it's a smaller image than yours.'

'Why do I have to look at this screen? I could just look at you.'

'The point is that both of us only look at the image of me.'

'OK,' she sighed. 'Now what?'

'I'm going to narrate to you what I'm thinking, what's in my head. And then you speak your thoughts about what you think about me.'

'So it's all about you?

'At the moment it's about my conscious awareness. You can have a go in a minute.'

I collected my thoughts. 'I see a man. He's young. He needs a haircut and a shave. I hope that this is fun for you and it works. The question is always: do I look how I feel?'

'OK, well I can see you, and, yeah, your hair has grown long, but you're still quite cute, and I don't know what's going to happen next. You're different from my other boyfriends.'

'I've got large dimples on either side of my mouth because I liked what you just said. I realise that I do want to please you and for this to turn out well.'

'You like to talk, don't you? And to think about things other than sex. I've been sexually active since I was sixteen, but we've only done it a few times. You'd rather be doing this.'

I can see from the periphery of my vision that she has turned to look at me. 'Sorry,' she said and turned back.

'Don't be sorry,' I replied; and I studied my face for the reaction to her honest comments. 'Maybe there's a slight anxiety around the edges of my eyes and I look a bit worried. My heart rate's gone up, that's for sure. It does feel like an interrogation and that I'm a sitting duck on this stool.' I paused. 'I've done this a few times now and I'm not sure I like it. It was OK when I was the observer.'

'That episode in the car was funny, wasn't it?

I felt my cheeks redden and looked for the signs on the monitor: it was hard to see much change in colour on such a small image. 'Yeah, I was lost in the moment, and you were there to bring me back to reality.'

'You pretended to watch yourself and then you wrote a book about it.' Melanie laughed a little. 'That is a weird thing to do.'

'Probably it is the definition of weird. I was hoping for wonderful as well.' I found that last remark too blunt to be honest. I saw that my forehead was furrowed, the creases perfectly visible on the tiny screen. I hadn't offered that insight to my interrogator and I realised that I was keeping things back.

'Sorry, mate.' She said it in a soft voice, as if I were one of her best friends. She probably kept up with all her exes and didn't banter about biblical quotes in cafes at awkward meetings with them. I believed she meant what she said. 'I hope you meant that.'

'Yeah, I did.'

A minute passed. The laptop made more noise than we did as we concentrated hard. I said: 'I'm extremely aware of the short distance between us and the concentration we each have on my face, my image, and what I might say next.'

I noted a change in my face. The lids of my eyes had drooped.

'You look tired,' she said, and resolutely stared at my face on the laptop, not turning to look at the real me once. 'I'm hanging in there, hoping something good will come of this.'

'If we stared really hard I wonder if we could make the equipment explode. Staring is a startling thing to do. War veterans develop the thousand-mile stare: a gaze into the distance that is free from the hell around them.'

'You look tired and serious and I think you would like this to stop.' Melanie breathed deeply. 'But I can keep going if you like.'

'Keep going,' I said. 'I am just here, existing, floating like an eyeball in space.'

'Yes, you have been taken over by aliens. If a bomb went off, you wouldn't notice.'

'Are you aware of being the observer?'

'Totally. My eyes are like lasers. It will be difficult to look at you directly. You seem like another person.'

'Yeah, you know what I look like?'

'Your reflection?'

'Bingo.' I said quietly.

We said nothing for a long minute.

Then in a small sweet voice she said: 'You can get your own back on me soon.'

But I stared even harder at my image and watched my mouth open as the words came out. 'This form of interrogation is exhausting. The scene I'm looking at, my face and the white wall behind me glowing in the monitor, isn't changing much. I am set at a passive level and just hanging in there. I can smell your perfume and the vanilla in the bowl. You have lovely legs.'

'Like Ruth's?'

'Much nicer.'

She suddenly laughed. 'Liar!' she said. 'Even the look on your face tells me you're lying.'

I stood up. Melanie stood up as well and looked at me. We

looked at each other as if we had been reunited in an airport arrivals lounge after years of absence.

'What do you think?' I said.

'Proper weird and very intense.' She paced the room. 'But it beats cleaning out the cowshed.' She put on her coat.

'Are you going?'

'No, it's cold in here.'

'The heating's on.'

'The heating's never on. You only set it for an hour then it goes off.'

I felt the radiator by the window. It was barely warm, but in a room made warmer by our body heat and the video equipment.

Melanie came over and stood right by me. She looked concerned. 'You're right here in the room, I can almost touch you, but it's like I'm watching you in prison; like you're someone else.'

'Welcome to my world. The idea is to explore the interior and exterior of a person.'

She gave me a warm kiss on the lips. 'Now it's my turn to be the guinea pig.'

She sat on the stool, wrapped up in her coat, and looked at the video camera. We set the stool forward a little so that her face was in frame.

I stayed behind the video camera, facing away with my back to her, and looked at her on the laptop screen.

'OK, so I see a princess, a pop star really, she is on a break, not beautiful, not ugly. Bit of a Cinderella character, wishes she could break free.'

She agreed. 'Teeth could be straighter. Nose could be smaller. I look like my Dad.'

I asked: 'How are you feeling? Can you say what you're thinking?'

'OK, I'm uncomfortable on this stool, my lower back aches, which means my period's due. My tits are aching as well, so don't touch them. I've really never had a boyfriend like you before and it is a bit of an adventure. But,' and then she stopped.

'Go on.'

'What do you think I'm going to say?' she asked.

'You're thinking it's all very weird.'

'Yeah, I'm like a stuck record. But this is weird.' She ran her hand through her hair and looked harder at her image.

'Your thoughts are a jumble. I've seen that look many times, there's less flicker in the eyes.'

'No, I am thinking of what to say, how to explain it, but it's complicated.' She exhaled deeply and watched herself in the video monitor as she experimented, shaking her head, sticking out her tongue.

'It's complicated because you're thinking that this isn't going to last too long, this relationship, fling, or whatever you like to call it.'

'Now it's interesting you say that.' Her voice was steady. 'Says something about you, doesn't it?'

'Yeah, it does.'

'Sheesh,' she breathed. 'This is like truth or dare. This is frigging intense.'

'It might be weird but it's not boring, is it?'

'Damn right. I can't believe I'm staring at myself. Normally I don't spend half this time looking at myself in a mirror. I don't take selfies of my fanny, either, and post them online like everyone else does, that's sick behaviour.' She sat up straight on the stool. 'I'm a farmer's daughter, but I'd rather be a movie star and wear furs and berets. I'm after my Prince Charming, like all the other slappers. That's what I'm thinking.'

'You're on to something there. Your tracksuit top suggests sport, but your fur coat suggests Cinderella and you *are* sporty; it's in your build.'

'Not at all,' she snorted. 'I ain't fat because I get up at six o'clock every day to get the cows in the parlour. This old top, I wore it today because that's what I had to hand and it's comfy.'

'I see you as strong, sporty, powerful, a bird, you could fly. But you're a delicate bird, no, not even a bird at all, more a butterfly. It's in your eyes, you have soft eyes.'

She shook her head. 'Butterflies are pretty, but they are weak. They are delicate: one touch can damage them.' Her expression changed to one of dismay and disgust. 'The more I look at my face, the less I understand.'

'That's interesting.'

'That's normal, isn't it? It's just looks like skin over bone, with a bit of makeup.'

She stood up, went over to the door and switched the lights on. We screwed up our eyes as the glare of artificial light hit us, until eventually we could see properly again.

'Truth or dare?' she asked.

'Truth,' I said.

'How many girls you got on the go?'

I turned the video camera off. She allowed me to hold her for a while and then we moved to the kitchen, where we sat down at the table.

'If you don't answer, then it's a dare.'

'You're made of tough stuff.' I looked her in the eye. 'It's just you. And that actually is the truth, as everyone knows.'

CHAPTER 25

BREAKFAST WAS NOT exactly a feast. We had tea in mugs. Frozen bread toasted too far until it was black around the edges. Solid honey and cold butter spread in chunks on the toast. We ate and drank in bed with the duvet around us because when the heating came on it turned off after only a few minutes. It was midday. We listened to the workmen and their machines outside.

'Poor old Mick,' I said.

'You liked him.'

'Yeah, I did. He loved that garage.'

'And he never twigged that you weren't real?'

I took a long sip of strong sweet tea. 'I think he got suspicious at the end, but no, I pulled it off.'

'You tricked him.'

'It was all innocent stuff. No one was hurt. It was a proof of principle for the project.'

Melanie got out of bed and walked naked to the bathroom. She had a larger bottom than I had imagined, and larger breasts.

'I'll have to put the water on if you want a shower.'

'I'll have a cold one, I don't mind.'

While she showered I got dressed and went downstairs to the studio. The video feeds from the bedroom were sent to the laptop in there. I tapped at the keyboard, moving files around to a hidden place on the disk.

Consciousness, I decided, was remembering who we were and what things were for. I was aware of the tapping noise from my fingernails striking the keyboard. I could also hear a high-pitched, two-toned sound passing the house: a police siren, I surmised. The sound changed and I remembered that what I was experiencing was called the Doppler Effect. You couldn't be conscious without memory.

I could hear Melanie moving about the bedroom. Then she went into the outer room. The window above my desk was being opened. I ran upstairs two steps at a time.

She was fully dressed, her shoes, coat and beret all on. The cold air seeped in to the room.

'Come here, you,' she said. We cuddled. There was a tear in her eye. 'You are lovely, but you are too much for me,' she said, and I knew that my little butterfly was going to fly away. I started to speak, but she shook her head. 'I am a farmer's daughter, and my Mum is the farmer's wife. I've got two brothers who are the farmer's sons. We have a happy family. We know our place.'

'Perhaps it's because you work with animals,' I offered, 'that you see things so clearly.'

'Yeah, animals are kinda dumb, but at least you know what you're getting.'

'I'm not saying that you're a dumb animal.'

'No, I know. But I am an object, with an inside and an outside, and I'm probably a machine, like you said, but to be honest I'd rather not know that.'

'Why is it a good idea not to know the truth?'

'Because it's easy and it's comforting. I'll go back to the farm and at weekends I'll return to Christos and his bookshop and even though I know it's all a bit silly, I shall like it.'

I let her go. She stepped back. I sat down on the chair where it had all started and looked out of the window at Mick's garage and imagined I was still in there, looking back.

'I'm aware that I damage others with my gaze.'

She laughed: 'Yeah, about that.'

I didn't stop her as she opened the desk drawer and scrabbled around until she found the video goggles. She also found an old set of earrings which she returned to the drawer. Gently she tossed the goggles out of the open window.

'The symbolic act,' I said, 'is very important.'

She came over and sat on my lap. 'I'm not going to leave a note like poor old Ruth did.'

'No need. You're doing this break-up very well.'

'My Mum once told me what to do, when I needed help the first time. She said I had to be brave. I cried for a day afterwards.'

'You didn't cry this time,' I said, but that set her off.

'I'm sorry,' she said, wiping her eyes. 'I wish this could work, but we're very different. But I do love you, and I'll never forget you.'

'I will never forget you, my little butterfly, not as long as I live.' I tried to stand up while she was still sitting on me, but it was awkward. She stood and disengaged herself, allowing me to walk across the room to the mantelpiece where my elephants were lined up in a row. I gave the largest one to Melanie. 'That's for you; if you hold it, it will light up and take on a little warmth.'

She took the elephant and put it in her coat pocket. Her eyes were streaming. She blew me a kiss and left the room. I heard the front door open. Her shoes clicked on the pavement as she walked away from the house towards the bus stop.

After some time, when my first emotions had subsided, I sent her a text message. An hour later a car pulled up and there was a knock on the door. It was a man with hair flecked grey in places and crow's feet under laughing brown eyes.

I made Father a cup of tea, and we sat down at the kitchen table together.

'How are you, son?' he asked.

'Battered, bruised, but I will survive.'

'I was worried about you. All that talk about conductors and pedestals, and then you had a bit of a turn.'

'I knew that would look good. I was playing a part. By then my wish to please the PI had taken over and the real Alexander had to disappear. I nearly lost myself, hiding in the shadows of the Hay Wain or out on the street.'

'It can become an addiction, stalking, following people.' Father continued to look worried.

I tried to reassure him. 'I know, it's not healthy outside the context of the work itself, and now the work is finished.'

Father smiled and grasped my hands. 'You are ontologically secure, you are a pioneer. You've developed the knack of disembodiment and returned to tell the tale.' He reflected for a moment. 'Melanie was a nice girl.'

'Dad, if we understand ourselves better, would we love each other more?'

His brow furrowed at the familiar term but he let it go. 'Why does that follow?'

'I don't know. People say that they want truth and to know how things really are, but I wonder.'

'Do you think of yourself more tenderly, with more amusement or with more hatred than before?'

I sat and thought about it. I had finished my project, I had my degree. I was on the hit list of a number of young women and on the regrets list of some others.

'More tenderly; I know how dangerous these investigations can be.'

'Good. Your Mother says that you're OK.' His big old face was pleased. 'I enjoyed your project.' He pulled out a fat brown envelope and slid it across the table. 'So, what's next?'

'I think I will go to Norway. There is the Art Nouveau museum in Ålesund: I've always been fascinated by it.'

Father got up and I found myself lost in his bear hug. He even kissed me on the head. Once I had heard his car drive off I opened the envelope. My parents must have donated at least a thousand pounds to my next adventure. I washed up the mugs and got ready to go.

ACKNOWLEDGEMENTS

M Y PROFOUND THANKS to Linda Bennett at Salt, for her diligent editing of the book, and for her masterly advice on writing.

This book has been typeset by
SALT PUBLISHING LIMITED
using Neacademia, a font designed by Sergei Egorov
for the Rosetta Type Foundry in the Czech Republic. It
is manufactured using Holmen Book Cream 70gsm, a
Forest Stewardship Council™ certified paper from the
Hallsta Paper Mill in Sweden. It was printed and bound
by Clays Limited in Bungay, Suffolk, Great Britain.

LONDON
GREAT BRITAIN
MMXVIII